CLOUD KINGDOM

FRED GRAY

VOLUME 1

Dear Michael

I hope you enjoy
this Fantasy adventure with it
and may you soar with it

Fred Gray

Published by Twin Press Publishing

5924 Peaceful Pass
Groveland, Florida 34736

ISBN: 978-0-578-50678-4

Cover design by 100 Covers, **www.100covers.com**

Interior layout by Mike Butler, **www.TorqueCreativeLLC.com**

Edited by Marsha Butler, **www.ButlerInk.com**

DEDICATED TO

God—*For the task and the journey*

Christopher and Leah—*For your inspiration*

Glen—*My number one fan*

Acknowledgments

I would like to express my gratitude to the many people who helped me as I wrote this book; to those who provided support, read, discussed, offered comments and assisted in its design, editing, and proofreading.

To Claudia Caporale, who befriended me at my first writer's group meeting, and showed me how to navigate this wonderful world of writing. Thank you for becoming such a beautiful friend.

To Mary Flynn, with special thanks for being my teacher, my mentor, and, most of all, my friend.

To Kelly Connelly for her support and encouragement.

To Kay for the time she has afforded me and my family, both immediate and extended, who supported and encouraged me despite the amount of time it took me away from them.

To my editor, Marsha Butler, Butler Ink, for her endless patience and professionalism and all the common stories of life that we shared.

To Mike Butler, Torque Creative LLC, for his fine layout and formatting of the interior of both the e-book and the print version, and for guiding me through the machinations of self-publishing.

To Matt Stone, 100 Covers, for his team's fantastic design work on the book's covers and his friendly, prompt, and professional service. Many thanks, Matt, for being willing to go the extra mile with me.

And, last but not least, I beg forgiveness from all those who have been with me over the course of the years whose names I have failed to mention.

Dear Reader,

I certainly hope you will be thoroughly entertained by this book. I invite you to slip into the life of your favorite character. Jump into his adventure, grab his power, and make it your own. Enjoy!

As always, I welcome your feedback or questions.

Sincerely,

Fred M. Gray III

www.fgrayiii@live.com

Index

Characters whose names
you might have trouble pronouncing:

Elephantous	(L-a-font-us)
Cloudasorous	(Cloud-a-sore-us)
Stratocloudous	(Strat-o-cloud-us)
Egosorous	(Ego-sore-us)
Rhinosorous	(Rhin-o-sore-us)
Tundrasorous	(Tundra-sore-us)
Pridosorous	(Pride-o-sore-us)
Qtrous	(Q-truss)

OTHER CHARACTERS:

Artie, the Elf Master of Cloud Kingdom

Stous, Prince of Darkness of Stratocloudous

Prous, General of Pridosorous

Queen Ciella, Queen of the Orange Realm

Lord Mason, Lord of the Rainbow Causeway

Liam, the Librarian of the Ancient Realm of Knowledge

Dragonfly, Princess of Purple Paradise

Nolan, New Prince of Tundrasorous

Q, Cloud Person

Clous, Cloud Person

Mars, Cloud Person

Lorous, Cloud Person

Renesha, Star Tunnel Creature

Florencia, Star Tunnel Creature

Greicius, Star Tunnel Creature

Kolya, Master Elder

Oda, Elder

Paola, Elder

Evil Eight:

Morgan

Droll

Ripkin

Spike

Lovonous

Venous

Lucian

Zererous

Realms:

Cloud Kingdom Magical

Purple Paradise Magical

Rainbow Causeway Magical

Orange Realm Monarchy

Ancient Realm Dictatorship

Stratocloudous Evil

Utopia/Tundrasorous Wasteland

Pridosorous Evil

Warasorous

PART
 ONE

*"The mind is an adventurous playground
but you must use it to keep it bright and clean."*

PART

ONE

TABLE OF CONTENTS

-Part One-

Chapter 1

-High Seas Adventure-

The scorching sun had dried the field and the thirsty grass scraped under Christopher's heels as he walked through the woods. Hearing a sound, he glanced up and spotted three kids headed in his direction. His heart skipped a beat as he ducked down quickly so as not to be seen. The Tara twins, Eddie and Liz, and their neighbor Jerry were always making trouble for kids in the neighborhood.

Not these three again. They stole my baseball glove and lied about it. Well, not today, Christopher thought. *I'm not in the mood.*

As Christopher waited them out, he became exasperated. *There has to be a better place to live where there are no bullies. Better yet, a place or a world you can go to and learn how to handle bullies.* Christopher loved pirates and thought they would know how to handle bullies.

After a while, Christopher cautiously peaked out. He saw no one so he gathered his things and hurried up the hill to meet his sister. As he passed the edge of the woods, he heard a sharp noise that stopped him cold. The three bullies stepped out from behind a cluster of bushes.

"Hey, Christopher," they called.

"Hey."

"What's in the backpack?"

"Nothing, Just stuff."

The tallest boy, Jerry, reached up and started tugging on Christopher's backpack, causing the side pocket to rip. Christopher struggled to get away as his belongings tumbled to the ground. The sun glinted off the metal pencil his father had given him. The pencil was very special; it bore his father's personal Navy seal. Christopher gasped when it hit the grass. The second bully, Eddie, snatched it up and ran. The third kid, Liz, grabbed the shiny black and chrome toy car that tumbled to her feet.

"This is sweet, thanks," she said and hurried off with

the others.

Christopher dropped to the ground, tears welling up in his eyes. *Dad just gave that pencil to me and now it's gone.* The tears rolled down his cheeks. *What am I going to tell him? He won't understand.* Christopher heard an authoritative voice coming from over the hill.

"Christopher, where are you?"

It was his sister, Leah, coming toward him with her typical sure-legged stride and broad smile. He quickly wiped his tears on his sleeve. Leah's smile always managed to make him feel better. Leah might have been the stronger of the two, but she would follow Christopher anywhere and do anything for him. She always looked up to her big brother.

"Sorry, I'm late. Were you talking to someone?"

"Nope, I just dropped my backpack."

She gave her brother a curious look. "Did you get all your stuff from your locker?"

"Yep!"

"Well, where is it? Remember, we're moving next week."

"How about you?"

"Done."

They took a shortcut home through the woods.

"I'm going to miss this old brick house," said Leah, as they approached the front door.

"Yeah, me too. It's the perfect driveway for playing basketball."

As they walked inside, their mom yelled from her office in the den. "Hi, kids! Come in here. I've got something for you."

Grinning at one another, they raced through the cluttered kitchen.

"Hi, Mom," Leah said.

Christopher dropped his backpack. "Hi," he said, hugging his mom.

"Okay, kids, we have a busy week ahead of us with the move. I bought you some special clear vacuum bags to put your clothes in."

"That's what you got us?" Christopher said glumly.

"So, let's get upstairs and start tearing apart those closets," Mom said. "The movers will be here on Saturday, so you can do your homework later."

"I'm going to get a snack first, then go up." As he grabbed his backpack with one arm, a few of his pens and pencils fell to the floor. His face flushed a bright red.

"Hey, what happened to that pouch on your backpack?" Mom asked.

"I...I got it caught on my locker, and it ripped."

Leah whipped her head around to give Christopher a knowing look. Mom didn't look convinced either. She reached out for the backpack and took it from Christopher. As if on cue, more of his belongings dropped from the hole as she grabbed it. Christopher tried to force a smile.

"I believe I can fix this. Empty it out and leave it in the corner. I'll sew it up. Get going, both of you."

"Okay, Chris what's going on?" Leah asked quietly from the kitchen so her mom wouldn't hear.

"Nothing. What are you talking about?"

"Brother! I want to know."

"Not now, okay?"

"I expect an answer tonight," Leah called as she ran upstairs.

Christopher put his head down and slumped upstairs. He closed the door behind him and sank on his bed. *I wish I knew how Leah does it. No one ever bothers her. Why do they think I'm so easy to pick on? Christopher shook his head. Maybe it's because I am.* He couldn't believe he'd lost his new lead pencil. The worst part of it was that he would have to tell his dad. He wouldn't understand because no one would ever pick on his dad, but Christopher just wasn't cut out to be a hero pilot like his father.

Christopher's eyelids grew heavy. He wavered in and out of a sleepy daydream. Questions drifted through his mind. What would it be like to be a strong, tough guy like Dad? Not a soldier or a pilot, but something like the adventurers in the books he read. Like a pirate? A pirate would never be bullied. Would Pirate Christopher find buried treasure? Would he be seasick when waves rocked his big pirate ship? What kind of ship would it be? Would it have great big sails? So many questions.

A parade of clouds moved lazily outside his window.

He imagined some of the clouds to be the vast, white sails of his pirate ship, puffed out by the wind and pushing him along to some awesome adventure. When the bright sun peeked through for a moment, the shape of the clouds appeared to change into a giant castle. Indeed, the sails became a giant, puffy castle. Christopher could make out the shape entirely. He even imagined waving flags on the towers, windows, and a drawbridge at the front. What kind of people would live in a cloud castle? Before he could even think up an answer, the sun peeked out again, shining directly in Christopher's eyes. He shut them, but not fast enough! Dazzling stars danced behind his eyelids. As Christopher blinked away the last of the dancing stars from his eyes, he realized he was somewhere entirely new.

"Wow!" Christopher's eyes blinked wide with wonderment. He wasn't feeling his soft, comfortable bed beneath him, but the hard, wooden planks of a ship's deck. He felt the planks creaking under him—the bed never did that—and heard the snapping sound of big, white sails catching the wind beneath them. He jumped to his feet and heard the loud clunk of his boots hitting the deck. He hadn't been wearing boots before. A strange, quizzical look came over his face when he looked down and noticed he was now wearing a paisley-patterned coat with two rows of gold buttons. He reached up and touched the brim of the tricorne hat that had appeared on his head just above the rim of his glasses.

He tugged at the coat sleeves, brushed the pants down, and readjusted the hat. No clothes ever felt this comfortable on him. *These are the clothes of a captain! Christopher felt right at home in his new clothes. He squared his shoulders and held his head high. As his perspective changed, he found himself more shocked by the change of scenery than his change of wardrobe. Christopher stood on the bow of a great wooden ship. The slapping waves rocked the* ship back and forth. Christopher smelled the salty sea air and surveyed the endless blue ocean stretched out in front of him. The enormous billowing clouds looked as if they were the pillars of heaven. Christopher held on tight as the sails buckled with the wind.

Where was he headed in these new clothes on a pirate ship? Christopher bubbled with excitement. His body was suddenly stronger. He felt mentally sharper and wiser. A great, odd, strange sensation flowed through him—courage. He felt whole finally and ready for a great adventure.

Chapter 2

Surprise Crew

"Captain!" a familiar voice came from behind him.

Christopher twirled around to see Commander Leah a few steps up in the wheelhouse of the ship. She took one hand from the ship's wheel to wave, locks of long red hair swirling around her dazzling smile and blue eyes. She was dressed much like Christopher in the slightly ragged garb of a pirate, but with the added flair of a single braid hanging below her red bandana that showed off its single feather. Christopher could tell from the look on her face that she was just as surprised as he was about being aboard this ship.

"How did you get here? Better yet how did I get here?" As she twirled, her feather tickled her nose, and her coat opened like a cape. "These are cool clothes," she exclaimed.

"I can't explain it, but it feels like someone or something heard my daydreams and answered them but I think we'll find out who soon," Christopher said. Feeling like the captain that he always wanted to be, he yelled, "I'm taking command of the ship! We've got work to do!"

Leah smiled. "I have a question, Sir."

"What is it?"

"Well, this is a beautiful place, but how are we going to get home? Is it dangerous here? What about Mom and Dad? Won't they miss us?

Christopher thought deeply for a moment. He didn't have the answers but he knew he had to appear confident. All of our questions will be answered when we find out how we got here. Now let's go!"

Leah saluted, "Aye, aye, sir!" *Where did this guy come from?* She tied the steering wheel down with a rope and tightened the knot to make sure the ship would stay on course, wondering how she knew how to do this. She then headed down the stairs to Christopher and followed close behind as he made his way across the deck of the ship.

Christopher stopped at the mainmast; the tallest, and most extensive on the ship because it held the largest of the sails. "This mast is where we need to go. The lookout nest is up there."

Leah fell in beside him. His eyes scanned upwards, tracing the mast, and by the time they landed on the unusually large crow's nest at the top, his head tilted all the way back. With one hand, he grabbed his hat to keep it in place. Beads of sweat appeared on his face. He reeled a bit from the height but knew that a pirate captain must be brave. Christopher gulped, wiped off the sweat, and began to climb.

A few feet up the mast, Christopher looked back. He saw Leah standing directly below with her hands on the rungs. Her head was also tilted all the way back and she looked every bit as nervous about the climb as he felt.

"Are you sure this is a good idea?" she asked. Before Christopher could reply, she answered the question herself, "Of course, it is. You're the captain! The captain is always right."

Christopher smiled and nodded. He had to be brave because people counted on captains. Leah wouldn't follow him if he looked unsure of himself, so he pressed upward. Before long, he could hear Leah climbing behind him mumbling, "...he must be right, he must be right..."

The higher they climbed, the more Christopher could feel the mast wobbling from side to side. The wind got louder and stronger; the bottom of his double-breasted paisley coat whipped open and flagged in the breeze. He was relieved when he finally made it to the top and climbed into the safety of the unusually large crow's nest. Captain Christopher reached down and gave Commander Leah a hand. Then, with her boots firmly planted inside the crow's nest, her eyes grew wide at what lay before them.

Chapter 3

– Treasure –

"What is that?" she said, pointing to the planks at their feet.

"A treasure chest!"

Christopher had hoped that his adventure would include treasure, but he never expected to find some on his own ship.

As he reached down to open the lid, Leah warned, "Are you sure you should open it? We don't even know what's inside."

Christopher stopped cold with his hand on the lid. He looked thoughtfully at Leah for a moment before a smile stretched across his face. "It could be the answers we're looking for and that's exactly why we have to open it! It could be something good."

Leah sighed. "It could be something bad too but you're

the captain!"

Christopher watched Leah cover her eyes, and then he pushed back the lid of the chest. It opened with a rusty creak. His eyes darted up long enough to see Leah peeking down through her fingers, and when he looked back down into the chest, he didn't see gold coins and jewels.

"Hmm," said Leah. "It's not bad or good, I guess."

The secret contents of the treasure chest were a pail of what looked like everyday dust.

Captain Christopher grinned. "What do you mean it's not good? The chest could be empty. Besides, it still might be what we're looking for!"

Commander Leah looked unconvinced. "Are you sure? Looks like dust to me."

"Sure, I'm sure." Christopher answered. "Now what should we do with it?" He reached into the pail and pulled out a handful of the gritty dust. Christopher held it up to examine it more closely when he felt a sudden breeze blow across his hand, taking the dust with it. He glanced toward Leah, who was trying to look innocent.

She shrugged. "Sorry, I couldn't help myself," she said with a grin.

Christopher was about to reprimand Leah for blowing the dust off his hand when he was cut off by a string of loud noises. *Snap! Sizzle! Pop! It sounded like someone had lit a handful of firecrackers on the main deck, but the beautiful colors and clouds of smoke that followed weren't from fireworks.*

Both Christopher and Leah leaned over the side of the crow's nest in anticipation of bright lights and colorful bursts dancing in front of them. When the noises stopped, and the wind carried away the colorful clouds, there was a completely new addition to the ship: a massive pool with a spiral waterslide filled the main deck.

"Ha!" laughed Christopher. "I knew this was more than dust. It's magic dust!"

They looked at each other in total amazement, eyes and mouths wide open. They couldn't contain their excitement and began talking at the same time.

Commander Leah nodded. "Man look at that." She pointed to the slide. "I want to try out that slide. Let's go for a swim!"

"Let's get the magic dust first," added the captain.

"Good idea, Captain. I'm sure we'll find plenty of ways to use it later." Commander Leah divided the magic dust in half and each of them put a share into their belt pouches before tying them off tight.

Leah turned to climb back down the mast, but her captain held up his hand to stop her.

"I have a better idea," he said, unhooking a long rope from the side of the crow's nest. He wrapped the end of the rope around Leah's waist…and yelled, "Hang on!"

"Wait, what about the magic dust? If we get it wet, won't that ruin it?"

Christopher smiled. "Nah, it's *magic dust!*"

With a brave jump, they went over the edge of the crow's nest and swung down toward the deck. Christopher released the rope at the perfect moment and they dropped into the pool with a splash.

They swam and played on the slide until dusk, and once the sun began to set went to look for a place to rest. They stopped in a beautiful stateroom.

Leah looked at Christopher. "Chris, this is fun, but we

are no closer to getting home than earlier today. What are we going to do?"

"Let me rest a moment and think. It has been one heck of an adventure."

Chapter 4

-Off Again-

Walking past the grand stateroom, Christopher and Leah spotted something strange lying on the bed. Christopher went closer to examine it, realizing it was a white towel that looked suspiciously like a fluffy animal. There was a little card placed at its feet that read:

"Welcome; I'm Elephantous."

Leah stepped closer, her eyes squinted, and her nose twitched up. "It looks just like an elephant," said Leah, stepping closer. "A towel elephant."

Christopher smiled. "A *towel elephant?*"

Leah reached out to touch the shape and pulled back a hand covered in dust. "*Magic* Dust," she said, looking at it closely.

Christopher thought back to how the dust had changed the deck of the ship and grimaced. "This might be a problem—"

He was cut off by a loud trumpeting sound as the towel elephant came to life, its long trunk coiling out to blow a low-pitched note. As the creature began to move, the sparkling lights returned in every color.

Christopher couldn't help but notice that the towel elephant was getting bigger—much bigger. Or was it that he and Leah were getting smaller?

"What's happening, Captain?" Leah moved her fingers and hands. "I'm tingling all over!" she yelled as the towel elephant's trunk reached out towards them.

"Run. Let's get out of here," Christopher said.

"I think we're shrinking!"

It was too late. The creature grabbed them both with its trunk and tossed them onto its back.

"I think we're in for a ride," shouted Christopher as the towel elephant lifted itself from the bed, circled the room, and carried him and his fellow pirate right out the stateroom window.

The towel elephant didn't stop there. It kept flying higher and higher, straight up into the clouds and beyond

Earth's atmosphere. Faster and faster it rocketed, right past the stars.

Appearing straight in front of them was a spiral of tiny multi-colored stars that formed a set of giant teeth. When they opened, they could see a doorway to a tunnel beyond the teeth. The mouth of the multi-colored star opened and closed rapidly. Cautiously, Elephantous moved forward. Swirling stardust and crackling sounds misdirected them and the giant mouth moved forward at lightning speed to grab them. Elephantous trumpeted for them to hold on as he zigged and zagged to avoid the star door. Too late. Christopher flew off, adrenaline shocking his body, causing his heart rate to accelerate. He heard his heart beat pounding in his ears as he headed straight for the door, screaming, "Leah, hold on!"

Elephantous reared up and twisted and pirouetted around at full speed. Charging at the star door, Elephantous trumpeted a blast of magic stardust at the door, hitting it head-on. The door slammed shut as fast as it had opened, but there was just enough time for Christopher to tumble through.

Christopher twisted and turned, kicking his feet and flailing his arms. "Help! Help!" Thoughts flew through his mind; most of them were not very pleasant.

Stopping short, Elephantous addressed Leah, "There is no way to know which realm he'll land in."

Leah screamed and pounded on Elephantous' back. "Who are you and what have you done with my brother? Let me go!"

"I am Elephantous, a magical transporter from the realm of Cloud Kingdom. I watch over all daydreamers in all the realms. Christopher's daydream was to go to another world to learn how to handle bullies. Today he was selected for his daydream to come true."

"I'll say it was his day! He's gone! What are we going to do?" Leah steadied herself, not wanting to cry or show weakness.

"First, I'll take you to Cloud Kingdom. I need you to meet a friend named Artie. He is an elf who rules in that realm."

"What! What is a realm?" Leah shouted.

"Cloud Kingdom is the central realm of all realms. When you walk in Cloud Kingdom, it feels like you have a spring in your step. Being there gives you a wonderfully peaceful and happy feeling." Elephantous tried to comfort her and nuzzled his trunk toward her. "The sunshine makes it so delightful. It is also the holder of all social and political events. The Council meets in the castle in the center of this realm."

Meanwhile back in Stratocloudous, arrows flew over Artie's head as he charged forward. The younger cloud people had no real experience in battle but were holding their own. The Stratocloudous creatures kept flying in and dropping cloud balls on them, while the cloud people created large cloud camouflage to redirect their aim.

They kept storming the mountain fortress on the outskirts of Stratocloudous. Stous's warriors were few in number there. Artie surveyed the battleground and determined that his spell would work. Casting a confusion spell, Artie watched as the enemy began dropping their cloud bombs on their own fortress.

Stous's lookout creature saw the change in the battle and sounded the retreat. As the creatures flew off, Artie and his team went into the mountain fortress. Inside, they found hundreds of cages made of lightning bolts with their tips buried deep in the ground. The tops had been left open so the Stratocloudous creatures could fly by and drop in their prisoners. Few cages were occupied.

"Mars, grab a couple of soldiers and retrieve the prisoners," Artie said.

"Alright, men. Follow me," Mars declared.

They were about to pull out their special gear to open the cages when Artie waved stardust from his fingertips. The pens opened.

"Thanks," yelled Mars.

Artie just looked over and smiled.

The prisoners were weak and confused. They didn't know where they were or who they were. Those were the lucky ones. The unlucky prisoners had been turned into soldiers for Stous's army and become brainwashed minions.

"Clous, take the prisoners to the rainbow causeway," Artie said, pointing toward a bridge of rapidly changing colors.

They all waited their turn for the proper color of the

rainbow. As the color slid by them, they stepped aboard and the army traveled back to Cloud Kingdom.

"Take me where? Talk to who?" Leah screamed. "I don't want to talk to anyone. Just take me to my brother."

"I'm sorry, I can't do that."

"Then take me back to that doorway where you lost Christopher."

"I didn't lose Christopher and that door is no longer there. Now, as I was saying, Cloud Kingdom is the most magical realm of all the realms where creatures like me, magical transporters, live among many other magical creatures,—teachers, warriors, and scholars."

"What are you talking about? I need my brother back! Please!"

Elephantous continued as if Leah hadn't said a word. "We're here to fulfill daydreamers' wishes and help dreams come true. We bring them to the kingdom from all over. Can you imagine a realm where no dreams came true? Oh, what a sad thing."

"Please, I just want—"

"In your realm, can you imagine if we hadn't been there to help the Wright Brothers in their dream of flight? How about Sir Isaac Newton's law of gravitation? Our magical warriors have been charged with protecting these gifts of *dreams since the angels of God roamed the realms. We are in battle constantly with the dark cloud creatures to protect these gifts. You must get to* Cloud Kingdom for safety and education."

"But I need to get Christopher back first!" Leah tried to jump off Elephantous.

"Whoa, little one." He held her down with his trunk. "You will. But to do so, you must begin at Cloud Kingdom."

Leah bowed her head and Elephantous felt steaming hot moisture run down his back. Her tears fell as she surrendered to her transporter's wishes. "Okay, if we must, but let's hurry up and get going." Trying to get Christopher off her mind, she asked, "Hey, how did you do that?"

"Do what?"

"Change your appearance and fly?"

"I can blend into my surroundings. My true appearance

can be a little frightening. But let me show you. I fly faster in my original form."

Leah felt Elephantous shifting under her weight. Turning into his true form, Elephantous was a hybrid of elephant and gorilla with just a touch of peacock thrown into the mix. He was about the size of a school bus in this form, but Elephantous could shrink in size if need be. His elephant-like features were sleek, strong, and muscular. His all-white skin was wrapped so tightly that all Leah could see was muscle showing through. He had the head of an elephant, a large trunk that folded up into itself, and his dazzling spiral tusk shone brightly only to be dulled by his great, wide, brilliant smile. His eyes were ruby-red orbs.

Elephantous's shoulders, limbs, and hands were gorilla-like. On his massive sides were large oval patches of plumage which, when looked at from an angle, appeared to be a hundred eyes staring back. With a flick of his plumage, massive wings appeared at his side. Its beauty would be the envy of a peacock. Golden bands were wrapped around his upper arms, ankles, and wrists. These golden bands held his magic.

"You are quite beautiful in this form," Leah remarked.

"Thank you."

With a flick of his plumage, he rocketed upwards through the dark space until they hit a gap that opened into crystal blue skies so dazzling Leah had to shield her eyes. The skies stole their brilliance from the sun. Once they were in the clouds, Elephantous skimmed along the puffy white surface and rolled, dropping Leah before soaring off. The pleasant breeze whispered comfort in her ears. More brilliant than diamonds, the sun warmed her face gently, igniting fear and warmth inside her at the same time. She heard an unusual creature call out in a deep voice, "Remember, Elephantous!" before disappearing into the clouds.

For a moment, Leah feared she'd fall all the way back down to their ship, but she landed on a flat bit of cloud that was as sturdy as any deck made of wood. And it was a deck. Looking around, Leah, saw that she was on a ship built from clouds—exactly like the wooden ship they'd left behind.

As awed as she was by the place that she'd been brought to, the thought uppermost in her mind was that she needed to find Christopher.

Chapter 5

– *Where To?* –

Leah turned around to climb the cloud steps up to the wheelhouse to get a better look at her surroundings. Out of the corner of her eye, she saw something move. It made her skin crawl. The steps echoed her climbing loudly. Without warning, a shimmering pile of stardust leaped, swirled, and bounced until it was upon her. She nearly jumped out of her boots when a creature that looked like a tiny person leaped out from the swirling, sparkling cloud.

"Come here!" shouted the creature in a scratchy voice as it ran across the deck towards Leah.

Commander Leah shrieked and ran up the cloud steps with the creature hot on her trail.

"Get away from me!" she shrieked, as the elf chased her in circles around the deck of the cloud ship.

Christopher flew through the star door. A blinking eye caught hold of his coat and ripped it from his body. He plummeted downward, his stomach swelling with fear. Lurching downward, Christopher felt a weight on his chest that made it harder for him to breathe.

Christopher finally landed on his backside, tumbled, and skidded into something hard.

"Ouch."

Dazed, he shook his head but heard the voice again.

"Get off me!"

Leaning on a rock, he dusted himself off and felt the rock wiggle. Jumping up, he looked around.

"Why did you hurt me?" grumbled the rock.

"I didn't mean to hurt you. It was an accident, for Pete's sake! Besides, I'm the one who just fell a million miles and landed on my rear end!" yelled Christopher. The moonlight reflected the shock in his bloodshot eyes when he realized he was talking to a rock. "Wait a minute, what are you?" Christopher demanded.

"You're the stranger here. Who are *you*?" the creature responded.

"My name is Christopher. What's yours?"

"My name is Greicius."

"What are you Greicius? A rock?

"Heavens, no!"

"Then what are you?"

"I am a char-asteroid. A sort of miniature asteroid."

"Have you always lived on this planet?"

"No. This star's atmosphere has robbed me of most of my power to move. I can only move inches at a time before my energy is drained and I must rest."

"What are your plans for getting off this star?"

Greicius let out a long sigh and groaned, "I'm stuck here."

"If I help you get out of here, will you help me?"

"Well…"

"Come on! You say you're stuck here. What will it take

for you to help me?"

Without warning, the sky ignited. A terrifying, screeching sound came over the distant hill.

"Whoa, what was that?"

"Someone tried to leave," Greicius said.

"What!" Chris's eyes widened.

"That's what I wanted to tell you. It's too dangerous. This star is full of bandits, lowlife drifters, and rogues, none of whom can get out."

"Has anyone ever made it out?"

"A chosen few. It's now a sport to be gambled on."

"You must help me," Christopher pleaded.

"Okay, but you will have to help me in return."

"How?"

"You must seek Princess Dragonfly of the Purple Realm and tell her of my fate," Greicius said.

Christopher placed both hands on Greicius and looked straight at him. "I promise."

"Okay, then you must take the path behind me, but first you'll need a weapon. I recommend seeing the Trader."

"Who is the Trader?

"He sells lots of rare, useful items and goods. To find him, go up the path to the right. Then go left to get to the blinking eye."

"Is that it?"

"Oh, and remember, timing is everything in this endeavor. Go now, for I must rest. Good-bye." Greicius fell quiet.

"Greicius, wait! Wake up! I have so many questions."

It was clear that Greicius was not going to speak again. Christopher bowed his head in resignation and started off on his journey. He followed the path to the right, just as the char-asteroid had told him. When he arrived at his destination, Christopher found that the trader had one eye in the center of his forehead and was the size of a leprechaun with ears to match. The trader leveled his eye on Christopher and stared intently.

"What happened to you, strange traveler? You're hurt,"

the Trader asked without hesitation.

"I came through that blinking star and landed pretty hard. It even tore off my coat on the way down. Listen, I need to get a weapon, but I have no money."

The Trader sneered. "Well, that makes it hard to buy anything, doesn't it?"

Christopher watched as the trader's gnarly hand reached the top of Christopher's head and pulled off his hat. The trader wrinkled his nose in a way that caused the creases on his face to pop out. Christopher had to try hard to kept himself from laughing aloud.

"No money, no sword," the Trader said.

Christopher cringed. "My hat is worth a sword." He grabbed the sword and handed over his hat. "Keep the hat."

"Thank you," the trader said. "Remember, timing is everything on this journey." Winking, he bowed to let the traveler pass.

"Yeah, you're not the first guy to tell me that," Christopher mumbled as he hurried off. He found the path to the blinking eye. The trail was a long winding curve and he had to keep to the center to avoid the ruts, roots, and potholes. The fern-like foliage reflected the light that lit the path. The aroma of the mossy grass that grew up the sides of the trees reminded him of home. He wished his sister was with him as she always made him feel strong and brave. Looking up, he noticed three figures walking his way.

"Hello," he said cautiously. He bowed his head, recalling his earlier experience with the three bullies.

The three creatures laughed, said hello, and walked on by.

Suddenly, they turned on him. Gravel crunched underfoot, as they scrambled to grab him. Christopher turned to face them. Too late! He felt the air change before the blow hit. He stumbled backward, dangerously close to the edge of the path, where the terrain dropped down into a ravine so deep he couldn't see the bottom. His knees buckled and he fell forward—out cold.

Christopher woke up with a headache and a swollen jaw. He lay there trying to piece together what had happened when he remembered the three creatures. He checked his pockets and found them empty. Christopher tried to stand. Feeling dizzy, he crawled over to a tree and lay down, tears rolling down his cheeks. He didn't know what to do. Staying with Greicius would be safer. His head slumped down—his plan would never work. Then, a shining glimmer of light penetrated his eyes. It was his sword. There it was, a few feet away, stuck between two tree trunks.

Christopher heard pleasant voices coming over the hill. Peeking around the tree, he saw two female creatures. "Help me, please," he tried to yell, but his voice came out in a whisper.

The female creatures shrugged and walked toward the tree. One pulled out her dagger while the other let out her claws and fangs. When they came upon Christopher, he saw the knife and tried to run but to no avail. His body wouldn't let him; he was frozen in terror. As one of the creatures bent down over him and he saw her claws and fangs, he fainted.

The creatures looked at each other.

"It's nothing but a boy creature and it looks like he needs help," said one.

The other creature cradled the boy's head in her lap.

Tapping his face lightly, Christopher's eyes fluttered open. Seeing the creatures face right next to his, he fainted again.

"My, what a squeamish boy," said the creature holding Christopher.

"Wake him up. It is dangerous out here," warned the other creature.

Complying, the creature holding Christopher slapped him hard in the face and woke him up. "It's okay. You're fine. Open your eyes and try to keep them open. Wake up. What's your name?"

Christopher relaxed for a moment before stuttering, "Who are you?"

"My name is Florencia and my friend is Renesha. Looks like you have had a hard day."

"My name is Christopher. Take whatever you want and leave me to my wounds," he whispered.

Renesha scowled. "You'd be dead already if we wanted anything,"

"Besides," Florencia added with a smirk, "whoever did this to you didn't leave you with anything for us to take."

"Okay, so what do you want?" Christopher whined.

"We're here to help if you can calm yourself down and tell us what you are doing out here," Florencia said.

"Three creatures jumped me while I was walking to the blinking eye."

"So you think you're getting out of here?" asked Florencia.

"Yes."

"We'll help you get to the blinking eye, but from there you're on your own. That's a suicide mission."

"I've heard the stories, but I must get out of this place so that I can find my sister."

Renesha looked at Florencia and shrugged.

Florencia looked at the darkening sky. "It's dusk, let's move."

Renesha wrapped her scarf around her neck to protect herself from the winds. "Christopher, where is your coat?" Renesha asked.

"I lost it in the blinking eye."

"Oh." Unwrapping her scarf, Renesha tossed it to Christopher. "Try this, it's better than nothing."

"Let's get going," said Florencia.

They heard something crunching along the path ahead of them—a creature coming down the hill towards them. The beast was smiling as he approached, his hands on the knife in his waistband behind his back.

The next few moments were a blur as Christopher's mind watched them play out in slow motion. Renesha threw Christopher behind her, and Florencia closed the gap between them and the creature, shielding Christopher from the creature. Florencia had her dagger out, and Renesha had claws and fangs at the ready. The oncoming creature leaped high in the air to go over them and behind Christopher. However, Florencia pounced on him in mid-air driving the dagger into his exposed belly. The creature whelped and disappeared.

Christopher looked at Florencia and Renesha and smiled, a single tear rolling down his cheek. "Thank you," he said.

"It's okay. He would have attacked us too."

The darkness hid their fears as they continued towards the blinking eye. Moonlight was scarce on the cloudy path.

"Let's get you to the wall," Renesha said. "It's close to the blinking eye."

Shivering, Christopher agreed. At the wall, they said their good-byes.

"Remember, once you get through the trees, it will open to the field," Florencia said.

Christopher held their hands. "Thank you so much for your help and restoring my faith that there is goodness in this weird place."

Smiling, Florencia and Renesha each hugged him, wished him well, and went on their way. Christopher broke through the wooded path into the starlit night. He saw a large flat area ahead. At the end was an enormous blinking eye. To the left was a large sewer pipe where a group of creatures was milling around. The odor that came from the pipe smelled like wet dog.

Christopher hid behind a wall, sitting with his knees up, resting his head on them. He fell asleep pondering his escape. The night passed, morning came and went. He woke up scared, hungry, and lonely. He needed out of here. His brain hurt from all the thoughts running through it.

He recalled the phrase that both Greicius and the Trader had used: "Timing is everything." What did they mean? He soon found out, as he watched the creatures try to escape by jumping through the blinking eye. To his horror, every one of them was killed or maimed.

The longer Christopher watched, the more he realized what Greicius and the Trader had meant. "Timing is everything." He closed his eyes and counted. *One one thousand, two one thousand, three one thousand, four one thousand. Open, close. That's the timing I need. Four one thousand.*

Christopher gathered his courage and watched the creatures jump. He found the place he needed to start, then ran straight for the star door in the blinking eye, knocking creatures out of his way as he ran. When he got to the spot he needed to be, he waited, and counted. "One, one thousand, two one thousand, three one thousand, three and a half one thousand." He took a giant step and somersaulted toward the doorway. He felt like he'd missed his mark but the door sprang open and he somersaulted in.

Just then, a multi-colored star tunnel opened and shot Christopher out.

"Captain!" shouted Leah from the cloud ship, "grab onto something!"

It was too late. Christopher fell through the clouds and plummeted toward Earth. He thought all was lost until something grabbed hold of his wrist and stopped his fall. Christopher looked up and saw an elf straining to hold him. The creature didn't look mean at all and stood on a sparkling magic carpet made of diamond stardust.

"Hang on, me boy!" grunted the elf, and with a sharp tug, he pulled Christopher onto the carpet beside him.

The elf frowned. "You don't want to fall to where the Stratocloudous live. Stratocloudous creatures are no good. No good at all."

"Thanks. Who are you? And where am I? Did I see Leah? What's going on? What have you done with my sister?" Christopher started to stand his ground and brought up his arms. "Where is she? If you've hurt her,

I'll—"

"Whoa, I did nothing to your sister. Hold tight and I'll take you to her."

"Not on your life! I don't know you." Christopher's fear turned into newfound courage. It was bubbling up to the surface and asserting itself. "Who are you? Where is Leah?"

"Please calm yourself," the elf said and fired stardust from his fingertips.

Christopher at once went silent and became very peaceful.

"Now, please hold on and I'll take you to her."

Christopher held on. The carpet pulled up right beside an amazed Leah and her tears changed into a smile. The elf reached out his hand to beckon her onto the carpet.

"No way! You chased me around this whole ship, now you want me to come aboard? What have you done to Christopher?" she said, crossing her arms.

"He is okay." The elf waved his hands and Christopher awoke.

"You both must have a lot of questions."

"You saved me," Christopher said.

The elf smiled. "Yes, I did."

Leah hesitated but finally reached out and took her brother's hand so Christopher could guide her onto the diamond-dusted magic carpet.

"Sorry about chasing you," chuckled the elf. "But I had just finished a scrimmage with the Stratocloudous creatures and I never let my guard down. My troops are on rest and relaxation right now. I was doing my final rounds when I saw your ship. Seldom do we see ships up here. My name is Artie." He reached out and shook their hands. "What kind of adventurers are you? Where are you from?"

"I'm Captain Christopher and this is Commander Leah. We are from Planet Earth, the third planet from the sun."

"Pleased to meet both of you. What brings you up to the clouds?" Leah looked up, "Well, first I...I was flying on an elephant that called himself Elephantous and.... and...he could change shapes and fly. Next thing, I lost my brother. Then I was chased by you…an elf!"

Cutting in, Christopher yelled, "We want to be pirates!"

Leah looked at her brother as if to say, "Where did you get the courage to want all this adventure?" She scowled instead and asked Artie with a scowl, "Do you know how we can get back home?"

Ignoring her question, Artie said, "Yes, I'm an elf. I guess the clothes should have given that away. I can help you. Let's be off to Cloud Kingdom! All your answers are there."

Christopher held tight to the magic carpet with Leah by his side as Artie guided it through the clouds. The elf was a strange creature and Christopher imagined that they were on their way to see even stranger creatures.

Stratocloudous echoed with Stous's bellowing for Egosorous, his second in command. Egosorous scurried to his side.

"Egosorous, get me eight of my best soldiers."

Moments later, standing in front of Stous were some of

the vilest and most dangerous beasts from Stratocloudous. Stous walked in front of them and inspected them from top to bottom and side to side.

"Good. Very good," he said. "Now, I want you all trained in stealth warfare. You will learn how to steal the souls of children when they start to dream. And you will learn how to turn those dreams into nightmares."

A wicked roar erupted, and his nostrils widened. The eight creatures nodded to their leader. A few of them laughed wickedly.

"Egosorous! Start their training immediately. You have three fortnights to get it completed." With that, Stous dismissed his lieutenant and the soldiers with a wave of his claw.

Egosorous quickly marched the line of creatures out of Stous's chambers.

Stous knew that six weeks was not much time to train soldiers in such a delicate set of skills, but he had great plans and his return to power could not wait.

Six weeks to the day, Egosorous marched his newly formed squad in front of Stous.

"Egosorous!" shouted Stous, "show me what they can do."

Bowing low, Egosorous sent his team out to ravage the nearest realm, Purple Paradise, a magical realm to the northwest.

Raising a staff capped with a strobing orb, Stous projected a view of his soldiers into the space in front of him. He watched as the squad dove in and out of distant hovels, laying waste to any interference as they stole souls and dreams. Once finished, the squad descended on Tundrasorous in precise formation and dropped the captured souls into waiting cages. Before he could turn to sit on his throne, the eight glided into a straight line before him.

"Ha! Perfect execution. Silent, quick, and deadly. Come to me, my precious eight. Egosorous, you are dismissed."

"But, Stous," Egosorous snapped, "you will need me to command my warriors—"

Stous scowled. "Who's warriors?"

"Yours, your highness."

"Be gone, sniveling creature."

Lowering his head, Egosorous backed out of the chambers rebuked by the snickering of the eight soldiers that followed him into the hall.

Stous grinned, exposing rows of sharp teeth, and then turned back to his soldiers. "Now, one at a time, come forth. I will bestow upon you a gift made by the fires of the stars that created the realms."

Morgan pushed his way forward to the front of the line and bowed.

"To you, Morgan, a tongue of fire that burns anything that it touches. Come." Stretching out his hand to Droll he said, "Ice shall be your weapon. Ripken, you will have this force field for the protection of all. Spike, what else but a lethal dagger that runs true?" Walking toward Lovonous, Stous eyed him up and down. "Yes, you will do nicely with this gift. You're now gifted with physical strength that has no equal. Venous, the sword is yours and there shall be none greater than you in all the realms. Lucian, the gift of invisibility shall allow you to move undetected." And with a flurry of his hands, Stous said, "Zererous, you will see what many others cannot; a sight that penetrates all obstacles shall be yours."

Each of the soldiers bowed as they received their gifts, although some looked far humbler than others.

Chapter 6

-*Cloud Kingdom*-

Christopher, Leah, and their new elf friend sped through the clouds until they reached a stretch of deep blue open sky.

"There are no clouds," said Christopher, "how are we supposed to keep traveling, Artie?"

The elf brought his magic carpet to a stop before answering. "We'll have to use a special route to get all the way to Stardust Alley in a reasonable time."

"What kind of special way?" asked Leah.

"The Rainbow Causeway."

"What's that?"

"Well," the elf continued, "the Rainbow Causeway is the primary form of transportation throughout all the realms. Lord Mason is the ruler of that realm. Each species sees a whole set of colors of the rainbow. Which realm they end up in depends on what color they jump on."

Christopher chimed in, "Do they make rainbows?

"Oh no," Artie said. "Lord Mason infuses special subjects of the Rainbow Causeway realm with a magical ability to collect rainbows, form them, and wield them together for transportation. Now, when there is no rainbow available, we must find two clouds that are about to fight. When they attack and explode with lightning, they leave behind a rainbow. All we've got to do is jump on the rainbow's red stripe, and it will send us back into the clouds. Lord Mason is always working on the rainbow to make it easier to use, as well as finding new places to go."

Commander Leah thought traveling by rainbow sounded dangerous—the worry and uneasiness made her dimpled and freckled cheeks glow red like freshly-picked strawberries. But they couldn't stop now; the adventure would end if they couldn't get back to the clouds. "Oh man, this is cool," she said, turning toward Artie with a forced smile. From the grin on Artie's face, Leah figured the elf could see right through her act.

Artie chuckled knowingly as Leah made her way over to Captain Christopher. She propped her boot up on the side of the magic carpet, straightened her back, and held her head high. She felt dominant standing among the clouds on a magic carpet and safe with her captain beside her.

Suddenly, lightning flashed and a faint rainbow appeared a short distance in front of them just as Artie had said it would.

"Hang on!" said the elf as he launched the sparkling magic carpet toward the bright red strip of light.

Both Christopher and Leah braced themselves just before the carpet struck the red bow of the rainbow. The sky exploded with twinkling stardust and millions of colors as the carpet and its passengers soared upwards. Artie's long, flowing hair covered his slightly pointy ears as the wind blew it straight back. His charcoal eyes shimmered between mystical and mischievous as they flew along the Rainbow Causeway.

Traveling on the Rainbow Causeway always invigorated Artie and caused him to grow to his regular height and size. Artie's leather armor covered his explosive chest, back, shoulders, and arms. He wore gloves and knee-high boots to match. His cloak flowed around him, giving him the appearance of flying. Artie's ashen goatee blended in with his devilish smile. His magical ability to change physical stature helped him in battle to become as large as needed against his opponents. He was smaller when traveling or when magical mischief was his lot.

An instant later, they were again flying over an endless stretch of fluffy white clouds.

"Before I take you to see my troops, I want you to meet someone."

"Meet who?" Christopher said.

"Patience, me boy," Artie chuckled.

Soon, they arrived at the castle in Cloud Kingdom. They walked into a chamber off the main entrance where a meeting was taking place. In attendance were Queen Ciella, Lord Mason, Liam the Librarian, and their new friend Elephantous. Elephantous sat against the wall watching everything that happened.

Christopher entered the chamber followed by Leah and Artie. Christopher swung his head around and noticed the large hexagon table where the Council had gathered. He walked around the chamber, his boots tapping out a musical cadence. The Council looked on, his shadow dancing across the walls as candlelight flickered from the chandelier.

Torch lighting surrounded each archway. Tapestries of ancient gods and their magical transporters hung on every wall. Christopher's nose twitched from the smell of burning beeswax. The moving candlelight reminded him of campfires at home.

"Good afternoon," scowled Queen Ciella and turned back to her meeting.

They continued to discuss how they would strike when Stous attacked again.

Suddenly, Captain Christopher turned in their direction and said, "Excuse me, but I do believe you are missing an important strategy."

The group went silent. Queen Ciella looked at Artie and asked, "Who are these creatures? Why have you brought them here?"

"Please excuse their insolence as they do not know

our ways," Artie said.

"That is no excuse; you had better teach them before bringing them into our meetings. I hope your reasons are sound for interrupting us."

"Please let us hear out these adventurers from the realm of Earth," Artie said. "Continue, Captain."

"I have heard some of your plans, but I believe that you have the advantage right now and you need to exploit it," the captain said.

"And what is this advantage, pray tell?"

"The element of surprise!"

The members looked at each other and said in unison, "What do you mean? Please explain yourself."

"We attack first. This Stous creature will never expect it."

A collective smile stretched across the group's faces.

"Your friends have some experience that we can use, Artie. Step forth. What is your name?" Queen Ciella asked.

"I'm Captain Christopher and this is Commander

Leah," he said gesturing for Leah to stand at his side.

"Well, since you both have titles I assume you may be addressed as such here. Please explain how you came to be here in this realm of Cloud Kingdom."

"We were on a pirate ship when we were trumpeted away by Elephantous," Leah said, pointing to the creature with a smile. "He wanted to fulfill the captain's daydreams but the captain fell off Elephantous and went through the tunnel of the blinking eye of multi stars." Taking a breath Leah continued, "Elephantous said there was no way of knowing where he would come out and I had to go to Cloud Kingdom where Artie could help me. On the way there, Chris was spat back out of the tunnel into our pirate ship. Artie appeared and saved him from falling into Stratocloudous." Shrugging her shoulders with upturned hands, her face seemed to scrunch up. "That is the simple explanation." She leaned over and whispered to Christopher, "Where did you learn about surprise attacks?"

"From my board game, War," Christopher boasted.

Queen Ciella nodded. "Alright. Let's get on with this meeting. We know if Stous gets out of Stratocloudous he will enchant them and lay waste to all young children's dreams and turn them into nightmares. Can you imagine?"

"How awful to go to bed with pleasant dreams and find yourself in a hellish nightmare," Lord Mason roared.

"I have heard of these spells," Liam said. "When you fall into your deepest sleep you are helpless for that moment and Stous can steal your soul. He takes it down to Stratocloudous and jails it there until he changes it into one of his minions who fight in his armies!"

"I have also heard rumors of Stous's Evil Eight," Liam complained.

"I too have heard rumors of them. They laid waste to some of Purple Paradise. It was a shame because everything and everyone who practiced the art of magic would go there to trade, buy, or learn magic," Lord Mason grumbled.

"We need to send spies to find out how Stous can move around with that tension bracelet on," Queen Ciella said.

"It has come to my attention that Stous has acquired a secret book of incantations. I have sent emissaries to find out if he has gleaned how to use the book. Unfortunately, I have lost contact with them," Liam mumbled.

Chapter 7

-*Playgrounds Are For Kids*-

Leaving the meeting, Artie took his newfound comrades to meet his resting troops. They flew across Cloud Kingdom, passing by many wondrous sights.

When they saw Liam's emissaries, Artie urged his magic carpet onward to catch up with them.

"There is something wrong with them," Leah announced.

"They look dead. But they're still moving," Christopher said. "The Evil Eight have taken their souls."

"All right, let's get out of here. We need to get a message to Liam," Artie said. "We must get Elephantous for this job." Artie sent out a magical message for all transporters to get Elephantous to come and see him.

Once that was done, they continued their journey. A few moments later, Artie's magic carpet stopped, sending Captain Christopher and Commander Leah tumbling off. They landed safely on a sheet of clouds, and when the two pirates looked around, they found themselves right in the middle of a wondrous playground made of clouds.

There were slides made from clouds held up by ladders of golden vines. Odd-looking children swung from the most unusual monkey bars made from a pair of monkey-shaped clouds that faced each other with arms interlocked. All around there were floating barrels, swings, and seesaws, all made from clouds, golden vines, and shiny things that looked like frozen bolts of lightning.

Christopher and Leah were awestruck and barely noticed when Artie landed next to them.

"Sorry about the sudden stop," the elf said with a shrug. "Do you like the playground?"

"It's more wonderful than any playground we've ever seen!" exclaimed Leah.

"And we've seen a lot of playgrounds," added

Christopher. "Our dad is in the military and we've lived in a lot of different places."

Artie smiled, looking proud of the playground and all its unusual offerings. "Come on," he said pulling them back aboard his flying carpet, "I want to introduce you to a friend. His name is Q and he's a cloud person. He'll be able to help you meet others like him and make lots of new friends."

"Cloud people!" Christopher and Leah said in unison.

"I can't wait to meet them," Leah added, looking at her brother.

Back onboard Artie's flying carpet, they zoomed through the city of clouds that seemed to stretch out around them forever. As they traveled, wisps of clouds filled their nostrils.

Leah laughed. "I have goosebumps on my arms, and it tickles all over."

"This cold mist is hitting me right in the face and it smells like cotton candy," Christopher yelled back.

Columns of clouds whipped by, leaving in their wake majestic buildings that pierced the floors of heaven. They were astounded by the beauty all around them. When the sun hit them, they sparkled like diamonds. What also caught their attention were the living clouds that looked like animals.

"Look!" squealed Leah. "That one looks like a dinosaur…and it's smiling at us!" She pointed to a cloud that was forming a shape like a tyrannosaurus.

They could see the large, grinning rows of teeth, even though they too were made from clouds.

"Oh, that's not a dinosaur," said Artie, steering around the large beast, "that's a cloudasorous. Most of them are friendly, but there are a few that will try to lead you to the Stratocloudous."

"Stratocloudous? What's that?" asked Christopher.

"Remember when I kept you from falling off the cloud ship? If you had kept falling, you would have ended up in the Stratocloudous. This is where Stous lives and reigns with his minions: Egosorous, Prous, Rhinosorous, and many more angry cloud creatures with evil powers. We have been locked in battle with Stous and his minions for as long as I can remember. Stous was king of Utopia, the most beautiful realm created. But all that beauty drove

Stous to believe he was God. Stous had to have absolute power and control over the people of the eight realms. Driven by his obsession for power, his greed and hatred, he tried to fill the growing void inside him with his evil deeds.

"Some of Stratocloudous is covered in fog that only Stous with his phosphorescent eyes can see through. The rest of the mountainous realm is dark and dead—nothing organic grows there. Domiciles are carved into the sides of the hill with narrow steps that wind all through the mountains. There are black caves with dungeons and large chambers for all sorts of wicked games. All you hear is howling, moaning, hissing, and shrieking. There is constant fighting between the minions with explosions and crackling fires. The smell of putrid sulfur, rotten eggs, steamed broccoli, and cabbage is everywhere. You don't want to go down there. You will have to be aware of them for they will want to do battle with you."

Leah and Christopher looked at each other a bit worriedly and nodded in agreement.

"Don't fret! I'll teach you how to stay safe…Once you meet Q and have a bit of fun, I'll get you started on your training."

Captain Christopher and Commander Leah looked at each other in surprise but both shrugged their shoulders. "Okay."

"There's Q now." Artie said, pointing to the funny creature just ahead.

Chapter 8

-*New Friends*-

It didn't take long for Christopher and Leah to notice that Cloud Kingdom was home to many different types of cloud people. They came in all shapes and sizes, tall and short, puffy and marshmallow-like. Some clouds even looked like ice cream cones and cotton candy. Some cloud people almost disappeared right in front of them. Their shades of white blended into the clouds, like pieces of a massive cloud puzzle.

"This feels like we are in a cotton candy world," Christopher said with glee.

Leah giggled. "I know I want to reach out and grab some and taste it."

Artie's friend Q was one of the skinny cloud people and had puffy bits of clouds for his head and the ends of his arms and legs.

Leah thought the cloud people like Q looked a bit like those cotton things you used to clean your ears. Artie brought the magic carpet to a stop a reasonable distance from Q and two other cloud people. The other two weren't the cotton swab type—one was a squat puffball and the other looked like a marshmallow.

"Shh," whispered Artie. "They haven't seen us. Let's sneak up on them."

Leah giggled quietly and Christopher smiled and nodded in agreement. The three crept closer, led by the elf, and at the last minute Artie jumped out right next to Q and shouted, "Surprise!"

Leah and Christopher laughed right alongside Artie, but when they realized the other, smaller clouds had run away from them and not because of Artie's scare, they got worried.

"Oh, I guess Clous, Mars, and Lorous decided to hide behind the slide," said Q. "They've never seen human creatures before."

"Come out and meet my new friends," Artie yelled towards the cloud slide.

Mars, Clous, and his sister Lorous poked their heads out and shook them. "Nope."

Christopher and Leah couldn't help noticing how comical their faces were, all scrunched up and worried.

"Here, I can fix this," said Artie, pushing up his sleeves.

With a wave of his arms, Stardust flew from the elf's fingertips and swirled around Christopher and Leah. A flash of light and a few sparkles later, and the two young pirates looked just like cloud people.

"Oh man, this is great!" squealed Leah.

"Wow!" added Christopher, waving his puffy white arm in the air.

Artie waved Lorous, Clous, and Mars over again, and this time the three cloud children happily approached for the introduction.

"Good to meet you Lorous, Clous, and Mars," said Leah with a small bow.

Artie broke in suddenly, "Oh my! I completely forgot to introduce Q."

Q chuckled. "It's fine, Artie. Allow me." Q couldn't help himself and danced with merriment as he introduced himself. "I'm Q and I'm three hundred and fifty-two years young. I like to play on the slide and the barrels, but my favorite thing of all is playing tag."

"We like playing tag too." said Captain Christopher, and that was enough to get all the new friends moving.

Chapter 9

- *Tag*-

The game of tag started and Leah and Christopher had a great time floating around just like the other cloud kids. They played for a long time, taking turns as "it" and running all through the cloud playground until Leah saw something that made her take notice.

Off to the side of the playground, there was a cloud kid who looked much like Q, except he was missing one of his puffy cloud arms and the other arm was overly large. Other cloud kids were near him, throwing cloud balls around him, playing keep away, and laughing at him. The cloud kid, Qtrous, chased the ball and yelled, "Throw it to me, throw it to me." The more they laughed and teased him, the harder Qtrous would try to get it, and the more he tried, the less he got it and the more frustrated he would become. Sweat ran down his face and tears burned his eyes. It aggravated him and his heart pounded harder and harder.

Leah felt so sad for the cloud kid that she didn't even see Artie walk up beside her.

"Oh my," he frowned, "that's Qtrous. Some of the mean kids pick on him from time to time. Doesn't look like he's having a good day," Artie said.

"We should do something about it," Leah said, heading over to the crowd surrounding Qtrous. Leah didn't like it when kids made fun of someone different.

Before she could get near, Qtrous started crying and ran away from the playground.

"Oh no!" Leah said, speeding up to catch him. "Wait, Qtrous! It's okay!"

She followed him down roads and into Wishbone Alley, moving deeper into Cloud City. While using her arms to keep her steady, Leah noticed she was losing Artie's magic and fading from a cloud kid to herself. Qtrous made a lot of twists and turns, and at one point, she finally lost track of him.

Did he go left or right? I'm pretty sure he went left! She turned left, passing under a sign that said, "Wishbone Alley" and noticed that the diamond dust ground was getting weaker and thinner under her feet. She remembered what Artie had told them about falling through to the Stratocloudous and stepped carefully with shoulders tight and nose curled. This was dangerous, but she was determined to find Qtrous and let him know he had friends who wouldn't bully him.

Chapter 10

-*Stratocloudous*-

Leah made her way carefully down the alley, but she couldn't find Qtrous. She was surprised when the sounds of Captain Christopher and Artie yelling her name sprang up from behind her. Caught off guard, she spun too quickly to answer them, stumbled, and fell through a weak point in the diamond dust floor.

"Oh no!" she shrieked, reaching for anything she could grab on to. However, there was nothing to grab and she tumbled downward. She fell for a few moments, trying to keep herself calm all the while, before slamming into a new layer of clouds with a thud.

The clouds weren't hard here, but they weren't as soft either. She rubbed her head as her vision slowly refocused. Wherever she was—Leah assumed it must be the Stratocloudous—it smelled horrible, like steamed broccoli, and the clouds were dark and angry looking. After a moment, she realized she was trapped inside of something like a topless cage, surrounded by bars made from lightning bolts.

It was not the unusual cage that frightened Leah but what was outside the bars. She turned in one direction and a creature charged the cage knocking itself out. The next creature took its turn as Leah ran to the other side. This creature got a claw through the cage, just missing her.

One of them—the scariest one of them all—looked right at Leah and said, "Get up, you hideous creature!"

Chapter 11

-Search Party-

"I didn't see where Leah went!" Christopher said nervously.

"Me neither," said Artie. "We need to put together a search party. If she fell through to the Stratocloudous, we must get her back quick! Now, before we get help, I want to tell you how to handle the Stratocloudous creatures."

"Okay, how?"

"Well, the first thing is you can't show fear no matter what," Artie said.

"How do I do that? From what you've said, they are huge, strong, and ugly."

"That's correct, but the secret is to stare them down, look straight into their eyes, and don't blink."

"Easy for you to say," Christopher said hanging his

head. "What you don't know is that I have a problem with courage and bullies. I'm not very heroic."

"Nonsense, I have seen you these last few days. You were both courageous and heroic. As for bullies, you didn't back away from me when you thought I was a bully and might have hurt your sister, Leah," Artie said.

"But that was different," Christopher said.

"Why?"

"Because she's my sister."

"Well, we're going after her, and we might encounter Stratocloudous creatures."

"Okay, okay."

"Buck-up, you can do this. Here's what you will have to learn." Leaning in, Artie grabbed Christopher's shoulders and spun him so that they were face to face. Pointing two fingers toward Christopher's eyes then pointing to his own eyes, Artie continued. "When staring them down, just look right through them and imagine what's on the other side. Another trick is to stare at them right above their head. Don't take in the ugliness, or their size. It's hard to do at first, but you can do it. Also, concentrate on thinking of not returning without Leah!"

Christopher and Artie hurried back to the playground to get more help and found Mars and Clous eager to volunteer. They were about to start planning their search when Qtrous came running towards them, still sobbing.

"It's my fault! She was following me, and she must have turned the wrong way and fallen through the clouds!" Qtrous said.

"Oh no, not Stratocloudous," Artie said.

"I want to help," Qtrous continued, wiping away his tears and putting on a brave face. "I can show you where she fell through."

Some of the other cloud kids started laughing when they heard this.

"What can you do? You can't even catch a ball!" some of them yelled. Others just chuckled and pointed.

"Don't listen to them, Qtrous," Artie cut in. "You can be a big help. You're very special with your one large arm. I'll bet you can stretch it out bigger than any other cloud person I know. And when you do, it works like a big sail."

"That's right," sniffed Qtrous. "That's how I'm able to

move so fast that people can't catch me."

"Great!" Artie smiled. "Well, now you can use that gift to help Leah. No more running away."

Many of the cloud kids looked skeptical, but Qtrous gulped and began stretching out his arm. Before long, he was catching the wind in the large arm sail.

Lorous pushed Christopher forward. "You need to go. That's your sister."

Shrugging his shoulders and lowering his head he said, "I can't fly, so how am I supposed to go?"

The group of cloud kids started yelling, "Go, Christopher, go."

Christopher shook his head and backed into the crowd, while Artie watched on.

Qtrous circled the other cloud people once, twice, and then zoomed through the clouds downward to Stratocloudous. The cloud kids weren't skeptical anymore, and he departed to the sound of all of them chanting together, "Qtrous, you can do it!"

Chapter 12

Rescue

Leah backed away from the huge, terrifying Stratocloudous creature that had yelled and growled at her. Surrounded by the lightning bolt bars, there was nowhere for her to run.

"You are very unlucky to land beside me," the creature hissed. "I am Stous and I rule all evil in the realms."

He stood up on his massive haunches, which held him to his full height of well over a story. Stous was a cloud creature that could shimmer into a solid creature. When he turned solid, his body turned into a crimson red that would shimmer back and forth with his cloud nature.

Leah's hair flew back as Stous moved his two large bat-like wings that sprouted out of his back. They were narrow at first and got wider and wider. Slim bones traveled through his wings to hold them up like sails on each arm. Veins created roadmaps throughout his wings from top to bottom and left to right. Each tip of his wings came to a point with a claw. His tail was longer than any anaconda snake and from the top of his dragonhead spouted three horns. The middle was the largest with the two side companions within inches.

Stous's eyes had no pupils. Phosphorescent sky-blue filled each eye socket. Dazzling white teeth jutted out through his gator-like mouth. His nostrils flared and puffed putrid violet vapors. His head was surrounded by a mane of white-and-bluish cloud-like feathers; his chin had matching whiskers. He had tiny muscular arms and large, scaly, razor-sharp claws.

"Now, you will come to me so that I can eat you!"

Just as Stous finished his sentence, Leah spotted something unusual floating toward her from the clouds above. She rubbed her eyes in disbelief as it got closer. It was Qtrous and he was moving as fast as lightning!

"Leah," he yelled, "Grab onto me and I'll…"

Leah gasped as Stous turned just in time for Qtrous to crash into his nose. But Qtrous acted quickly, jabbing the stubby part of his missing arm into the huge creature's phosphorescent eye. Stous roared and fell to the ground, blinded by Qtrous's quick thinking. Leah grabbed onto the cloud kid as he whizzed by and held on tight as they soared back up to Cloud City.

As they climbed higher and higher, Stous roared after them, "This isn't over! I'll hunt you down, you freak! And you, you redheaded creature, I'll find you, too! There is no escaping Stous!"

When they reached the safety of the City of Clouds and the playground, Qtrous landed gently on the stardust lane, setting Leah down beside him.

Captain Christopher grabbed Commander Leah and hugged her tightly, remorsefully asking, "Are you okay?" while the sounds of cheering cloud kids filled the air.

"You did it, Qtrous, you saved the day!" they yelled and danced.

Artie stepped up and raised his hands to get everyone's attention.

"Qtrous didn't just save the day," he smiled, "he saved our friend Leah. Everyone here should remember that there is meaning and reason to everything in God's world. Just because you don't see the reason, doesn't mean it's not important. It doesn't matter if someone is different; God uses everyone who says yes to Him. Qtrous here is special, and he was able to use his differences for something amazing." With that, Artie raised his hands again and shouted, "Now let's hear it again for Qtrous!

Leah woke and found herself sitting in the closet surrounded by plastic bags with clothes in them. She stood, shook her head, and marched into her brother's room. Christopher was daydreaming so she poked him in the arm. "Wake up! Oh my gosh, what just happened? Come on, wake up!" Leah said.

Christopher's eyes fluttered open and looked at Leah.

Christopher sat up and said worriedly, "Are you okay? What's wrong? What are you doing in here?"

Leah couldn't contain her excitement. "Don't you remember?"

Christopher flinched at Leah's prodding finger but was much slower to wake up. He grumbled and rubbed his eyes, shook his head, and swatted his sister's hand out of the way. His stomach was upset and he didn't look well.

Leah recognized the look on her brother's face and stepped back.

"Captain! You look like you're going to throw up!" she was so caught off guard she didn't even realize what she'd called her brother.

Hoping to avoid a mess, Leah ran into the bathroom and grabbed a towel from the rack. She ran back to Christopher and found him standing and stretching.

"That was weird," he groaned. "I felt seasick for a second like I was just on a large ship."

"You were! Are you feeling better now?"

"Yeah," he grinned. Then Christopher looked thoughtful. "Wait, what did you call me?"

"Huh?" Leah said.

"You called me Captain!" He smiled. "Did you have the dream, too?"

"You remember!" Leah squealed. "The flying carpet, the elf named Artie, the funny cloud people…and the one that everyone laughed at—"

Christopher cut in, "Who saved you?"

"That's right! I fell through the clouds, and there were these terrible, mean-looking cloud creatures. Then he flew out of nowhere and saved me. His name was Qtrous!"

Christopher nodded and his face looked puzzled.

"How could we dream the same thing?"

"Only one explanation," Leah said slowly, "it wasn't a dream."

The siblings looked at each other and smiled before yelling in unison: "Oh, man, this is great!" Christopher looked at Leah and frowned. "We have to keep this to ourselves for now. No one will believe us and we don't know for sure what happened."

"I wouldn't know what to say anyway because I don't know what happened."

Mom's voice cracked the air, "Kids come down and help me get ready for dinner!"

Climbing down the stairs, fear gripped Christopher when he remembered about the bullies and the loss of the special pencil his dad had given him. Also, he remembered how he failed Leah. At that moment, he heard something in the back of his head: "It's not easy at first, but you can do it." He could swear it was Artie's voice.

Reaching the kitchen, Leah glanced at Christopher with a smile on her face.

Christopher silently shook his head and mouthed, "Stop it."

Dad walked into the kitchen to see Leah and Christopher sitting in their self-assigned seats. He kissed their Mom and took his own chair.

"How is everyone doing?"

The chaotic voices of Christopher and Leah hit him at the same time, jumbling up all that he heard.

"Okay, calm down. One at a time."

"I got all my books home today, Dad."

Leah yawned. "And I got most of my room ready for the movers."

"Good, you know Saturday is the day for the movers, so everything from school has got to be home," said Dad.

Later that evening, Christopher and Leah discussed every way possible to get back to Cloud Kingdom without coming up with an answer.

"I'm tired. We'll come up with something by morning," Christopher said.

Going to their rooms, Christopher was again hit with the fear of telling Dad about the bullies and the loss of his lead pencil. Again, he heard Artie's voice in his head saying, "It will be hard at first, but you can do it. Just like facing the creatures in Stratocloudous."

Dad yelled, "Okay kids, get ready for bed and we'll be up to say prayers."

Mom and Dad were in the living room, the lights low and peacefulness in the air.

Mom grabbed Dad's hand and guided him to the sofa. "We need to talk about Christopher."

"What about?"

"Well, he came home with that new backpack ripped. I asked him what happened and he simply told me a fib. Then he forced that smile of his when something happens and he is just too embarrassed to talk about it. But I do think you need to say something to him."

"Alright, I'll talk to him," Dad said in the clipped military voice he was known for. "When we say prayers tonight, I'll broach the subject."

The room was lit by moonlight when Dad walked into Christopher's bedroom. The gold bars on his uniform glimmered in the moonlight as he took a seat on his son's bed. "Is there anything that's bothering you, son?"

"No, why?"

"Well, your mother knows you fibbed to her about your backpack."

"Aw, Dad it was nothing. I got into a little pushing around with the boys that wanted my stuff. My backpack got ripped, that's all."

"Son, you know you can tell me anything. It's okay."

"Thanks, Dad. It's cool."

"Good night. I love ya. Pleasant dreams, son."

As Dad started to close the door, Christopher said in a soft squeaky voice, "Wait." With a lump the size of an apple in his throat, he said, "Dad, I do need to tell you something."

Leaning in the doorway, his father said, "Go ahead, son." He noticed his son trembling. "What's wrong, son?"

"Well, you know that special lead pencil you gave me. It's gone. Someone took it."

Dad stood to attention and asked, "How did you let that happen?"

"Well, I didn't let it happen. They ripped my bag and when it fell to the ground the other kid took it."

"How many were there, son?"

"Three. Two guys and one girl."

"Why did you let them get so close to you to take it?"

"I don't know. It happened so fast."

"You let a girl take something from you too?"

Christopher squeezed his eyes closed. All he could see in his mind was the girl running off with his shiny race car. Stuttering in silent sobs, Christopher answered, "Yes."

With a military clip to his voice, Dad asked, "Where is

your code of honor, son?"

"I…I don't know, Dad. I'm so sorry I lost your pencil."

"Go to bed, Christopher. We'll discuss this in the morning," Dad said closing the door behind him. He paused, then stuck his head back in and said, "Son, I am afraid that this looks like a pattern starting. Remember when the Tara twins and their neighbor Jerry stole your baseball glove?"

"It's not, Dad. Honest." Chris watched his Dad shake his head as he closed the door behind him.

PART
TWO

*"The best part of being on a journey
is knowing you're on one."*

TABLE OF CONTENTS

—PART TWO—

Chapter 1

– *The Egosorous* –

Darkness rolled across the landscape deep in Stratocloudous. An awful sulfurous smell like rotten eggs floated through the air.

Huge, harsh mountains of grey and black clouds flashed with jagged lightning and the air filled with the crackling sound of thunder. Flashes of lightning danced over the faces of a dozen creatures crowded together in an open expanse of the angry-looking clouds.

In the middle of it all, Stous stomped back and forth. The fierce cloud creature reached up and rubbed the spot where Qtrous, a cloud person who turned out to be far more heroic than he looked, had poked him in the eye destroying it and leaving the socket empty. Remembering the way Qtrous had swooped in and rescued the red-haired girl he'd captured angered him even more. With a grunt, Stous kicked a flurry of dark cloud balls from under his foot and watched them soar through the air, gaining in size as they flew. The largest cloud balls started to glow red like fire, whistling and spinning, and finally hitting another cloud creature, causing a loud explosion.

"Ow!" the other cloud creature shouted as the explosion knocked him on his tail. The other cloud creatures circled him, laughing, and pointing. The one known as Jealousy shouted in a shrill voice, "He got you good, Egosorous!"

The fallen creature stood back up, wiping himself off and grumbling, "You can't do that to me."

"What was that, Egosorous?" growled Stous. "Did you say something?"

Egosorous stepped back and swallowed hard before shaking his head. "No."

"Thought so. Now, back to this Qtrous problem. I want him captured and brought to me. He owes me an eye and I will have my revenge."

The cloud creatures nodded quickly in agreement, Egosorous making the biggest show of all.

"And I want that red-haired girl too. My dinner was cut short by that lousy cloud person and I intend on finishing it. Now fly and find them!"

Chapter 2

-*Return*-

Leah woke up covered in sweat. Even her clothes were wet, and her sheets were on the floor as if she'd be thrashing in her sleep. Jumping out of bed and feeling her way down the hall, she headed to Christopher's room. The door squeaked as it opened. She tiptoed to his bed and reached over to poke him in the arm.

"Are you awake? Get up! I remember what Elephantous said to me. He said he watched over all daydreamers in all the realms. Are you awake? Come on!" she whispered, shaking her brother.

Christopher rolled over and grumbled, "Go away. Go back to bed."

"Chris, I recall. When Elephantous flew away, he said, 'Remember to call upon my name!'" Leah, angry now, jumped on Christopher. "Get up!"

Christopher's eyes flew open. "Stop jumping on me. What do you want? What time is it?"

"I don't know. It's late."

Christopher rubbed his eyes.

"Remember how it all started with a towel that was folded into an elephant?" She ran into the bathroom and came back with a towel, tossing it on the floor. "Now what's next?"

"I remember that he grabbed both of us and threw us on his back and flew us up into the atmosphere. That's when I went through the tunnel," Christopher said. "And I don't know if I want to go back there. That was scary."

"Oh, come on," Leah said.

They sat on the bunk bed and thought about what happened the first time they were taken up to Cloud Kingdom. Leah nodded and closed her eyes. A few minutes went by but no ideas came to either of them.

"This isn't working."

"It has to! It just has to!" Leah cried, hopping up and down on the edge of the bed. "Please. Christopher. Get us back there, Captain! I need to thank Qtrous for saving me!"

"Don't worry, I'll get you back there," he said and

turned away.

Leah saw his grimace and all hope disappeared. "I guess we'll never get back."

Christopher perked up and put on his most determined face. "No! I must get you back there. I'm your captain." He scanned their room looking for more clues, anything that might give him some idea as to how to return to the city in the clouds. When his eyes landed on a small drawstring pouch, they lit up. He leaped from the bed and ran to the bag. "I've got it!" he yelled, hoisting it into the air.

Leah looked at the pouch, and it stirred a memory. Something about blowing dust from her brother's hand? Leah walked over to Christopher and took the pouch from his hand. She opened it and peeked inside, seeing a few handfuls of sparkling magical dust. The sight stirred something else in her memories, and she looked back at the bed. "Take some of the dust," she said, holding up the pouch. "I think I have an idea."

Christopher reached into the pouch and pulled out a small pile of the sparkly stuff. Leah grabbed the white towel from the floor, while Chris examined the powder in his hand. She threw the towel on the floor at his feet and smiled.

"Now, open your hand. I remember Elephantous telling me as he was flying away to just call upon his name if we ever wanted to go back!"

Christopher opened his hand above the towel and his face flashed with recognition. Just then, Leah blew on his hand, and the dust rained down over the towel.

"Elephantous!" shouted Leah.

A string of loud noises erupted from the towel: *Snap! Sizzle! Pop!* The room filled with sound, flashing lights, and clouds of multi colors as if someone had lit off a handful of firecrackers…but Leah and Christopher both knew that these were not fireworks.

"It's working, look!" shouted Christopher. "The room is getting bigger!"

Leah looked around. "No, Chris…my hands are tingling again and we're getting smaller!"

Just as the siblings shrank down small enough to fit through their bedroom window riding atop Elephantous, a gust of wind blew through the room and stirred everything inside. Their homework papers swirled around them, toys rattled on the shelves, and the white towel began to rise from the floor. Within seconds, it took on the shape of a strange, white elephant.

"Here we go again!" said Christopher.

Elephantous looked at them and trumpeted through his trunk. With a single graceful swoop, the creature scooped Leah and Christopher from the floor and headed out the window. Round and round they flew, circling their house several times before shooting straight up towards the clouds.

Chapter 3

–Aero and the Amulet–

Artie, the Elf, sat quietly on his magic, diamond-dusted carpet as it hovered inches above a long stretch of puffy white clouds. He was lost in thought. Staring off into the distance, he thought about how the war for dreams and nightmares was taking a profound toll on all the realms.

Suddenly, his magic carpet bounced, and Artie's eyes opened wide. It jumped a second time, nearly sending the elf flying off the edge. He turned around and saw his two pirate friends, Leah and Christopher, sitting behind him.

Artie smiled. "What took you so long to get back?"

"What do you mean?" asked Leah.

"Yeah," Christopher cut in, "we've only been gone a few hours."

Artie raised his eyebrows in a puzzled look.

"Are you kidding?" he asked. "It's been over two years. Sad to say, but I stopped looking for you guys months ago. I thought you wouldn't come back at all. Thankfully, Elephantous always knows where to find me."

"Yup. He's accommodating...for a towel." Leah giggled.

Artie smiled for a moment and then shrugged.

"Anyway," she continued, "I want to find Qtrous so I can thank him for saving me. Do you know where he is, Artie?"

"Not exactly, but I will help you find out. There's someone I need you to meet first. It came to my attention that on your previous adventure, I never properly introduced you to Aero." The elf jumped down from the carpet and beckoned for the siblings to do the same.

Christopher and Leah looked at each other and shrugged, then stepped off the mat.

Artie smiled. "I know you're confused, but let me finish."

With that, he snapped his fingers and his magic, diamond-dusted carpet began to shine even brighter.

Bright sparkles rained down from the carpet as it swooped around, stood upright on its corners, and bowed.

"Whoa!" shouted Leah. "Are you seeing this?"

"Yeah, and I don't believe it either." said Christopher.

"This is Aero, my diamond-dusted magic carpet. He says he's happy to see you again," Artie said.

With a little wiggle and a wag, Aero rubbed up against Leah and then Christopher like some sparkling, magic dog.

"It's good to see you again, too, Aero." laughed Leah, petting him gently.

"And now I have a present for both of you." Bringing his hands together in a thunderous clap, he created a colorful explosion of shimmering light so bright that Leah and Christopher had to shield their eyes. Emanating from Artie's hands, the light dissipated outward throughout the realm. When they looked again, Artie was holding a beautiful, golden object out towards them.

"Is that some Cloud Kingdom jewelry?" asked Christopher.

"Sort of," Artie said. He pulled the figure into two

halves and handed one-half to Christopher, the other to Leah.

They both looked at their piece of the object, puzzled.

"I know," said Artie. "It's hard to tell what these are when they're separated and inverted, but when you put each half together, they form a triangle with small openings at the points of the triangle."

Leah and Christopher put their halves together and noticed the shape.

"The opening is for the spirit to enter the amulet and move around inside," Artie explained. "But that's not the important part when it comes to making it work. For the amulet to do its magic, you both need to unite your halves just as you're doing now."

Leah looked at the amulet, then to Artie. "But it's not doing anything now."

"It will if you say the right words. With the pieces together, you need only say, 'One, Two, Three…Cloud Kingdom.' You will be transported from wherever you are to Aero and me. As you know, going home is not a problem because all our realms have portals to travel to your realm."

"Awesome!" said Christopher. "Easier than trying to remember how to use magic dust."

Artie giggled. "Much easier. The secret to the amulet is that you each must have the correct half of the charm and invert it correctly for it to work. It's part of the protection built into it. In fact, if someone else were to get their hands on both pieces and put them together without you, they would be hurled down into the depths of Stratocloudous."

Captain Christopher looked at Commander Leah and nodded. Using his most heroic voice, he proclaimed, "We thank you, Artie the Elf, for this sacred gift. We pledge ourselves to our special missions here in Cloud Kingdom."

"Aye, aye, Captain," Leah agreed with a sharp salute.

Artie smiled and imitated Leah's salute with a giggle. "You're both quite welcome. Now, let's go find Qtrous."

Chapter 4

-Gold and Diamond Sparkles-

"We made a lot of new friends the last time we were here," said Leah as they flew through the clouds on Aero. "Maybe they can help us find Qtrous."

"Good idea," said Artie. "We'll need to scour the kingdom to find everyone who might know him. Let's start with the gates of the castle since a lot of cloud people hang around there."

Captain Christopher nodded in agreement and Artie steered Aero off in a new direction. The magic carpet swayed gently side to side as they flew and a wake of sparkling stardust kicked up from either side. The waves of golden sparkles caught Leah's eye, and she reached out to put her fingertips into the shimmering current. Leah found herself giggling for no reason.

"Chris!" she yelled over the rushing wind. "Try this. It

tickles your hand and makes you giggle."

Christopher stuck both his hands into the stream of sparkling dust, but he didn't giggle. Instead, tears started flowing from his eyes, and he quickly pulled back his hands.

"Chris! Did you get hurt?" Leah shouted.

"He's not hurt," Artie smiled. "That's just the stardust. It makes little girls giggle, and young boys cry."

"That's so weird," Leah said.

"If you touched diamond dust, it would be just the opposite. You would be the one crying. Besides diamond dust and golden sparkles will do a lot more once you know the spells that command them."

Leah looked at the current of sparkling stardust with a new appreciation.

Chapter 5

-Old Friends-

"Now hold on," said Artie, "we're about to reach the Rainbow Highway. We'll need to bounce into the red bow to get to the castle."

Leah and Chris held on tightly as Artie steered Aero directly into a vast, colorful rainbow. They collided with what was a solid wall of colored light, but as soon as Aero connected with it, they soared off as quick as lightning. The adventurers whipped around all the familiar colors of the rainbow and several others they'd never seen before. Leah and Christopher stared in amazement at the sheer beauty surrounding them.

Ever the expert pilot, Artie focused on the sky ahead. He waved his hand and magic dust flew from his fingertips. Aero began to spin and glide slowly toward the red portion of the rainbow. The magic carpet connected and the world flashed with a vivid red light.

Christopher and Leah both blinked their eyes as the bright color faded, soon realizing that they were floating above a moat filled with water. The moat surrounded a massive wall of clouds that stretched on for miles; the only break in its shape was a giant, golden drawbridge directly beside them.

"Hey, Artie." a voice called down from above. "Where did you find our long-lost friends?"

Christopher and Leah both looked up and saw Clous, a cloud person they'd met on their last adventure, sitting on top of the gates.

"Hi, Clous." the siblings yelled in unison.

"We've been waiting a long time for you two to come back," Clous continued. "You're here just in time. You might be able to help with something."

"Actually," Leah cut in, "we'd love to help, but I need to find Qtrous first."

Clous frowned and said, "Well, then your timing is perfect. Artie, I need to talk to you about something."

"Just come down here and start talking sense," Artie said, waving to his friend.

Clous jumped from the gate and floated gently in front of Aero and his adventurous riders. "Well, it started a few years ago…" Clous began rattling off words too quickly to understand. "After Qtrous helped save Leah, he wanted more fun and excitement. The rescue gave him a lot of courage and he ran off looking for adventure. He joined the battles for dreams and nightmares between Stous and all the realms."

"Sounds like he might have gotten a bit too much courage," Artie remarked.

"Maybe," continued Clous. "We haven't seen him since he left. Both Q, Mars, and Lorous went off to try and find him. I was chosen to wait here at the gates in case Qtrous came back on his own. All of us have been saying a special, silent prayer that you two would come back to help us."

"Well, we're here now so, let's get going."

"I agree that we need to help, but let's make a plan first," Artie said.

Chapter 6

-*Captain Takes Command*-

Christopher knew it was his responsibility as captain to determine their course, so he looked up at the sky to get his bearings from the stars. The pattern of stars above him looked different from anything he was used to.

"Wait a second." Using the forefinger and thumb of each hand, Christopher made a triangle holding his hands up towards the heavens. He looked between his fingers and saw something strange: a bunch of stars forming the shape of a triangle with a swirl inside. "There!" he shouted, pointing toward the shape in the sky. "The stars will lead the way."

"I think you're right, Captain," said Leah. "I'm not sure why, but I feel it too. Qtrous is over there somewhere."

Artie looked at his pirate friends with admiration and smiled. "You've got it, Captain," said the elf with another salute.

An instant later, Aero and his passengers were zooming in the direction of the triangle of stars. They flew for what felt like hours, and then those hours turned into days. On the third day, Aero began to shake and stutter, rocking back and forth as if they'd flown into invisible waves. Before anyone could react, something hit the bottom of the magic carpet and sent it rolling.

"Hold on!" shouted Artie.

Christopher grabbed Leah's arm tightly and held on to the side of Aero with his other hand. The carpet flipped and rolled, making him dizzy. Seconds later, all Christopher could see was that they were plummeting downward, and fast. Aero the magic, diamond-dusted carpet tumbled down into a cavernous valley. They yelled as they held on tight, trying not to be thrown off. After falling several minutes, they landed hard at the bottom of the valley, bouncing against the puffy surface and sending Christopher flying off. Aero bounced again, this time sending Leah soaring off into the clouds. On the third bounce, Artie barely managed to hang on, but he was finally able to get Aero back to normal. The elf steered his magical friend Aero back towards Leah and Christopher and jumped off.

"Are you guys okay?" he asked, lifting them off the ground and dusting them off.

"I'm fine," said Christopher. "It's a good thing the ground is made from clouds up here."

"I scratched my arm," said Leah, "and I probably have a couple of bruises, but I'll be okay."

"Let me see," said Artie, looking closer at Leah's wounds. He reached over to Aero and took some of the magic carpet's diamond dust in his hand. Artie spat on his hands and rubbed them together.

"Gross!" Leah said.

Artie then spoke some magical words that she didn't understand and reached out to grab her arm. When she jerked it away, he gently pulled it back and spread the concoction on her wounds. She flinched, but as soon as the salve touched her injuries, she felt a huge difference.

"Hey, what are you doing? Wait, that feels good."

"It's okay," said the elf with a grin.

Leah looked down, and the scratches and bruises were gone.

"Nice trick!" said Christopher.

"Yeah," Leah added, "thank you!"

"Now, what happened?" Christopher continued. "Is Aero okay?"

Artie looked over at the carpet and Aero once again stood up on his corners and nodded.

"Well, then why did we crash?" Artie asked him.

Aero shrugged, diamond-dust sprinkling down from his edges.

"Hmm," said Artie. "Judging from these clouds and how far we fell, this must be Stratocloudous." Artie shuffled to the side, clapping his hands. "Quickly...get aboard. We need to get out of here before we are spotted. I pray it isn't too late."

Egosorous watched from a perch high above while several of his minions gathered around him. He was a long, thin dragon-like creature. His length was about the size of three train cars and his body resembled the underbelly of an alligator. He also had a gator's short, stout arms, and legs. What was unusual was his head. It looked just like an ordinary horned dragonhead but with gator teeth, wide nostrils, and beady eyes. His wings were in perfect proportion to his body and tail. Unlike an alligator, Egosorous could breathe huge streams of fire, and his power was quite beautiful to behold. When he prepared to attack, his whole body turned to fire from the inside out, from tip to tip. Even his talon claws would burst into flame. Flames glowed all about his body. All you could make out was a ball of fire that looked exactly like a flying flaming dragon. It was an awesome sight, frightening and deadly.

"That was a nice hit, boss," said Jealousy. "You brought 'em down good."

"Yes, it was," replied Egosorous without taking his eyes from his prey in the valley below. "And now that they're down there, I'll show Stous that he can't bully me and get away with it."

"How are you going to do that?"

"First, I'm going to capture them and their foolish magic carpet. Then I'll use them to lure that Qtrous down here. Once I've got them all, I'll parade them right through Stratocloudous in a cage." Egosorous's grin showcased a row of razor-sharp teeth.

"When Stous sees that, he'll know who's the best around here."

Chapter 7

- *Plan and Attack* -

"Stay down," whispered Artie, "and I will go see what's ahead of us." The elf walked over to the edge of a cavernous wall and peered over carefully. What Artie saw gave him a chill.

Carved into the cavernous walls were caves and stairs that lead into a vast chamber. Inside, Artie heard a loud rumbling, "I want that red-headed creature." Artie was so close he heard the echoing of the magical chain that tethered Stous to Stratocloudous. The smoldering sulfurous smoke rose above the wall and irritated his nose. He knew this confrontation was going to take all the strength of his new adventurers.

After another moment, he noticed something moving in the distance. Getting a closer look, Artie saw Queen Ciella and her army marching on Stratocloudous. Artie was startled by the sight of her army and ran back to the siblings and Aero.

"It's going to take teamwork and timing for us to get out of here. Not only is there a nasty-looking Stratocloudous creature standing between us and the nearest rainbow, but Queen Ciella's army is posing to attack."

Captain Christopher and Commander Leah looked at one another in disbelief.

"Well," Captain Christopher said, puffing out his chest, "teamwork is what we do best!"

"Yeah, we're pirates." Commander Leah added. "And our lives depend on working together. Right, Captain?"

Captain Christopher nodded with a knowing grin.

"Our lives will depend on this." Artie said.

The adventurers huddled together and discussed the situation. Captain Christopher and Commander Leah thought carefully about how to handle the creature.

"Let's deal with the creature first, then help Queen Ciella and her army," Artie said.

After a few moments, they had their plan.

"Okay, let's go over this one last time," said Artie. "Leah, you're going to be the decoy and draw the creature's attention. Once it's running, Christopher will battle the creature and take it down."

"Wait, are you sure I can't be the one who battles the creature?" Leah asked.

Artie raised his hands, "We have to work as a team, remember? You're already the most important part of this plan, Leah. If the creature isn't distracted, Christopher doesn't stand a chance against it, even with my help."

"What are you planning to do, Artie?" asked Christopher.

"I'm going to confuse it," the elf smiled. "As soon as it starts chasing Leah, I'm going to run in the opposite direction, giving her a chance to get away. We don't want that thing catching any of us!"

"What do I do once it stops following me?" asked Leah.

"Aero will wait around the corner. You'll jump on Aero and pick us up for a quick escape."

Leah nodded.

"One last thing," Christopher cut in. "You haven't said how I'm supposed to battle this thing. If it's as big and mean as you say it is, I can't just wrestle it!"

Artie chuckled. "No, you wouldn't want to do that. As far as Stratocloudous creatures go, this one isn't the most dangerous. It's young and not very bright but you still don't want to be around it for too long."

"So, what then?"

"You're going to make it vanish. Poof! Gone!"

"What?" Christopher's eyes went wide. "And how am I supposed to do that?"

Artie grinned slyly, "Since this isn't an old, strong creature, you can make it disappear with some of that magic dust you brought with you. You need only sprinkle it in the creature's eyes and he'll vanish."

"Are you sure that this magic dust will work?" Christopher blurted out.

"Oh yes, young creatures have yet to learn how to use their inner powers," Artie replied.

"You make it sound easy. You said it's big," Christopher said doubtfully, "so how am I supposed to reach its eyes?"

"Before your sister and I distract it, you're going to climb that wall," Artie pointed toward a high point on the cavern. "She'll lure it past you. You'll have to jump onto its back and climb up to his head as it runs by."

Trembling inside, Christopher looked a little less sure of the plan.

"You can do it, Captain," Leah said. "Remember swinging from the crow's nest of the ship? It's just like that!" *Without his pirate garb, he is less confident,* she thought.

Christopher felt the fear starting to compound his trembling with the shakes. He tried to think positive thoughts and realized he felt stronger the longer he was in Cloud Kingdom, so he smiled and nodded to his sister.

"Alright!" said Artie. "Let's get into position!"

With that, everyone went to their starting positions. Christopher climbed the wall and thought, *This isn't so bad.* Leah prepared to dash out in front of the creature, although she was more than a bit worried since she still hadn't seen it.

"Okay," said Artie, "one…two…three…GO!"

Leah sprang into action and ran around the corner towards the creature. It looked in her direction as soon as she got near, and the beast was more frightening than she'd ever imagined! The cloud creature was at least as tall as a school bus, and if it hadn't been made of dark, gloomy clouds, it would have weighed as much. Its eyes glowed like red lightning, and its mouth was filled with jagged cloud teeth. Before Leah knew it, the creature was running her way. Leah spun on her heels and ran in the opposite direction, leading the beast right towards Christopher. She could feel the creature getting closer and closer; its long legs making it much easier for it to catch up.

"My turn, you ugly thing!" she heard Artie shout just as she came near Christopher's wall.

She turned and saw Artie pop from around a corner with a flash of stardust. It looked like the creature didn't like that display at all, as it turned its mighty head and bounded toward Artie. Leah followed the plan and ran towards Aero.

Behind her, Artie led the confused Stratocloudous creature past Christopher. Christopher hesitated. His mind went blank. The air filled his nostrils with sulfur.

Dizzy, he no longer could see Artie or Leah. His breath came so fast he couldn't even scream for help. The next sound he heard struck his cerebral brain—the sound of Stous's screech.

Out of nowhere, Stous swooped down on Christopher and shot a fireball at him that nearly knocked him off the wall. Hanging on by his fingertips, Christopher tried to scale the wall but the slime made it hard. Over his shoulder, he saw and felt Stous. His feet slipped on the slimy wall. Stous was coming in for the final blow.

He heard Leah yell, "Watch out."

Christopher shook his head and lunged upwards. His feet gained traction and hurled him up the wall. He regained his composure and his position on the wall, grabbed his sword, and drew it back ready for Stous. Stous dived in and attacked just as Christopher brought the sword forward and clipped one of Stous's talons. Quickly readjusting himself, Stous reached out with both talons and grabbed Christopher's sword and flew off with his new trophy. Fearfully, Christopher remembered he needed to jump onto the Stratocloudous creature's back.

Within seconds, Leah abandoned the plan and flew

in on Aero, leaped off, and onto the Stratocloudous creature's back, sending Aero for Christopher. Leah climbed one scale at a time until she reached the top of his neck. Grabbing her pouch of magic dust, she emptied the contents right as the creature turned to bare its fangs.

Leah gasped as the jagged teeth closed around her, but they faded just in time to miss her. A second later, the entire beast faded away and she dropped through the air. She landed on Aero with a thud as Christopher guided the magic carpet gracefully along the cavern floor.

Looking around and seeing Stous had gone, Christopher took in a deep breath. He was still shaking but couldn't believe he had lost his sword—the one he'd traded his hat for.

"You did it!" shouted Artie as Christopher stopped Aero right beside him.

"We all did it, especially Leah," said Christopher worriedly as he held out his hand to Artie. "Teamwork, remember?"

With a curious look, Artie nodded, and Christopher pulled him onto Aero.

"Thanks. Now, let's help Queen Ciella and her army," Artie said.

Aero and the companions flew up to the top of the cavern wall to check out what progress Queen Ciella had made. Artie saw Queen Ciella and her armies ready to invade Stratocloudous.

Stous stomped back into his war room, "It's time to take the battle to those nosey do-gooders." Stous shook his mangled claw. "Egosorous!" The minions scattered as Stous swiped the maps off the table and pounded his fist down, almost breaking the table. "Where are you?"

Moments later, Egosorous materialized in the chamber and cowered before Stous.

Stous threw Christopher's sword at Egosorous. "Hang this on my trophy wall and summon the Evil Eight. I want to talk to Morgan."

"Yes, Master."

Within moments, the Evil Eight descend into the war room.

"Listen up, Morgan, I'm charging the Evil Eight with an attack that will get rid of these do-gooders once and for all. Gather round. No one shall know of our plan but you. Now, go." Stous smiled and watched his elite forces take flight. *Now, I will be ready for you, my friend, Artie.*

The strike, as Christopher put it, would be preemptive. Stous had big plans in the works for stealing the dreams from creatures in all the realms. He would do it all at once. Timing was everything. For Stous's attack to work, all realms had to be attacked at the same time. This would maximize the element of surprise. While Stous was using a small contingent to attack the Rainbow Causeway, the rest of his armies would attack the realms.

What Stous didn't know was that Queen Ciella was marching to attack that day. Also, he had no clue that Egosorous had tracked and attacked Artie which had brought him and the adventurers down to Stratocloudous.

Stous had just put the final piece of his battle plan together when the first firebombs were lobbed into the caves. Stunned by the sudden attack, Stous thought quickly. He called for his general, Prous.

"Recall all our armies immediately! We need to protect

Stratocloudous."

"But, sir, they are about to make the biggest strike ever."

"I said recall them, General Prous!" Stous bellowed.

"Sir, if we don't strike now, our chance to replenish the army all at once will never come again."

"I won't repeat myself again. Recall the troops. Without Stratocloudous, we will all die."

"Speak for yourself. You are the only one tethered to this realm."

"What did you say?" He struck Prous with an energy cloud.

Struggling to rise, Prous yelled, "I still believe it is a mistake."

Stous stomped out of the room. *I will have to put an end to him soon.*

Stous's troops circled above each of the realms, ready for the attack signal; instead they saw the signal to retreat. In confusion, some of Stous's forces retreated while others attacked.

Queen Ciella battled Stous for hours. Her armies were on the verge of victory when Stous's reinforcements came swooping in, wave after wave dropping cloud bombs on her army. With the tide turning, Queen Ciella realized she was trapped. Seeing her cut off from her forces, Artie and the adventurers decided to join the battle. Artie turned and looked at Captain Christopher and Commander Leah.

"Wait here for a moment."

With a flurry, stardust circled them, and Artie was gone. Captain Christopher looked at Commander Leah, clasped his hands behind his back and paced nervously. Leah reached over to grab her brother to calm him, but she couldn't stop him from trembling.

"Where did he go?" Leah pleaded.

"We're going into battle, and we're wide open for an attack," Christopher shouted. "We have no weapons to even fight with."

She stared into Christopher's eyes. "Christopher, you can't continue to freeze all the time. People depend on you."

"Don't you think I know that!" he growled.

"Well, what are you going to do about it?"

"Don't you worry your little head about it. I'll take care of myself; besides you're not perfect."

"You better or you'll lose your life," she said as a tear burned her cheek.

When Artie returned he knew something was amiss with the two adventurers. "Is everything okay?"

Looking at each other, they both replied, "We're worried for the queen."

"Me too, but now we can do something about it."

Artie handed Captain Christopher a sword and Commander Leah a longbow with a quiver of arrows. "These weapons have been forged from the stars of the eight realms after God infused them with life. Now, they will protect you against any weapon in any realm if you supply the power of faith to them. The faith in God that infused them, yourself, and each other will continue to make them stronger. Now, let's go sneak up to Stous and his troops. Follow me!"

As they traversed the mountainside, they kept close

together and out of sight. When a soldier of Stous's flew straight down upon them like a dive bomber, Christopher drew his sword and Leah nocked an arrow. The weapons tingled in their hands as they adjusted to the new owners. The power of the weapons became theirs and they moved like an expert swordsman and champion bowman.

Drawing the bow all the way back, Leah let her arrow fly true as it hit the dragon in the heart. Artie turned to see it coming straight for him when Christopher ran up the mountainside, leaped high above the dragon's head, pirouetted, and came down with the final blow that took the dragon's head clean off. Artie smiled at both the adventurers, saluted, and they entered Stous's crypt together. They crept up behind Stous as Christopher and Leah grabbed the last guard.

Artie snuck up behind Stous with his sword drawn and dropped onto Stous's back. The elf put the sword to the creature's neck and whispered into Stous's ear, "Call off your army or your head will be the first to go!"

With a sudden loud screech, Stous's minions retreated. Queen Ciella's army let out a tremendous whoop and holler.

"Back to the Rainbow Causeway," Queen Ciella commanded.

"Until next time," Artie uttered in Stous's ear. Taking one of Stous's horns in his hand, he snapped it off. The crack echoed off the chamber walls.

The minions stopped momentarily when they heard the horn snapping and the sudden cry of pain and foul screeches that emanated from Stous. Stous felt weak and stomped around in a circle, holding his head where Artie had just stolen his horn.

Artie held the broken horn over his head. "I got this close once. I'll do it again. Think about this next time you want to take the dreams and souls of the young from the realms."

Artie snapped his fingers and Aero gathered Artie and the adventurers up. Together, they flew off to safety.

Upon the ledge high above, Egosorous watched it all.

"Boss! Boss!" Jealousy cried out. "Did you see Stous let them go? He lost one of his horns to that crazy elf. That's all because you brought him and those two pirates here."

Egosorous gave the minion a sideways glance.

The minion continued his rant. "If Stous finds out, you're dead!" In response to the look that Egosorous gave him, he added, "Don't you worry; your secret is safe with me. I'll take it to my grave. Right, boss."

"Oh, Jealousy, I know I can count on you. Prepare to leave. Tell the others it's time."

As Jealousy turned to go to do his master's bidding, his exit was cut short by a fireball launched from Egosorous's smoldering mouth.

"You thought it wise to laugh at me? You'll be in your grave sooner than you think." The demented laugh of Egosorous could be heard echoing off the cavernous walls.

Chapter 8

– *Fun* –

The adventurers soared toward the nearest rainbow, Aero leaving a faint trail of diamond dust as they flew away from where they'd faced the fierce Stratocloudous creature. Artie looked back curiously as Leah and Christopher each raised a hand in the air and slapped them together.

"What's that all about?"

"It's called a high five," replied Leah. "It's part of working together!"

"Yeah," Christopher added. "We do it when a plan comes through, or when teamwork makes something good happen."

"Wow," said Artie, "I like that! Can I try?" Artie's magical mischief side jumped out and wanted to play.

"Sure!" said Leah, raising her hand. "Come on. Smack it high!"

Artie wound up his arm as if he was about to pitch a baseball and then slapped it hard against Leah's. When their hands clapped together, a shower of tiny sparks erupted between them.

"Whoa," Leah gasped, "that feels weird."

Suddenly, she began to sparkle all over. Her skin turned puffy and white, and her arms and legs became rubber-like and drooped down to the ground, skinny like straws. Her red hair stayed the same, but now it was falling over a cloudy face that only a mother could love. She was turning into a cloud creature. A nasty looking one at that.

Christopher didn't know whether to be angry or to burst out laughing. When Artie chimed in, giggling, "Oh my, now that is funny," it sent Christopher over the edge, and he couldn't control his laughter.

"Hey!" Leah shouted, "It's not funny, you two. Now fix me."

Artie stifled his giggling and snapped his fingers. In a flash, Leah was back to her usual self. She turned a pouty glare on Artie. "Next time, give the Captain the high five and leave me out of it!"

Chapter 9

Rainbow Travel

High above, Egosorous still looked on. He watched as the elf and his two little friends soared away after not only escaping but destroying his fierce minion, helping Queen Ciella, and disgracing Stous by taking one of his horns. Egosorous growled and mumbled, kicking at the clouds and baring his teeth.

"They shouldn't have made me mad!" he shouted. "Now, I'll lay a trap that captures them all! They're not going to get away again!" Egosorous leaped into the air and began to soar higher and higher. Once he was sure he was high enough his prey wouldn't see him, he started to follow the little pests and their flying carpet.

Aboard Aero, Artie explained the current state of the war to his friends. "The battle over dreams and nightmares is intensifying, and we must be more vigilant."

"That was intense fighting with those creatures,"

Christopher said.

"We needed to help Queen Ciella. Without our help, she could have been trapped and lost that battle," Commander Leah remarked.

"We must find out how Stous plans to remove all the dreams at the same time and stop the nightmares once he replaces the dreams," Artie said.

"Did you see that huge shadow in the sky?" Christopher said.

"What was it?" Leah asked.

Concern and worry wrinkled Artie's face. Artie felt a cold shiver. "Whatever it was, it's gone now."

High above the castle in Cloud Kingdom, the shadow grew bigger.

"Now, split."

Morgan, Ripkin, Venous, and Droll turned 180 degrees and headed out to find Artie.

Lucian yelled, "Follow me" and turned his invisibility shield onto the three that followed him.

They glided down onto the top parapet of the castle.

The moonlight shone on the small windowed chambers above them. Passing, their shadows dimmed even the muddy panes of glass and reflected shadowy images on the parapet walls. The walls, spattered with the past blood of warriors, gave way to the smell of the fresh kill at their feet. Lucian, Zererous, Spike, and Lovonous crept through the castle looking for the doorway that would take them into Artie's chambers.

"Zererous, turn on that x-ray vision of yours and find that doorway," Spike whispered.

Light emanated from certain patches of the mud-brick walls, giving away the secret chambers that lay behind them.

Zererous smiled. "Check out those spots over there."

Each one took their leave, checking for the chamber they were tasked to find. With the rising of the moon, the night cooled and the day's heat condensed on the castle walls, escaping like tears. Reaching the dimly lit walls, they searched for the secret opening. Lucian felt around the brightest and noticed a raised spot. He pressed it and a sudden burst of chilled air escaped. He had found it. He called everyone over and they gathered around a doorway that appeared before them. The seal sparkled with magic dust.

"How are we going to get in there?" Lovonous griped.

"Get in where?"

The question floated from around the corner. Spike grabbed his dagger. Lovonous brought his finger to his mouth and let out a, "Shh." Zererous froze in place while Lucian became invisible.

Clous marched around the corner repeating his question when he looked up to see Stous's minions. Spike drew near to Clous asking, "Are you alone?"

Stuttering, Clous nodded vigorously. "Yes."

Lucian appeared behind Clous and grabbed him. "If you want to live, you'll do exactly what we tell you, got it?"

Clous again nodded vigorously.

"Good." Lucian motioned for Spike to lead Clous to the doorway.

As Clous turned toward the door, Spike gave him a quick kick in the butt. Clous landed on his knees and crawled to the door.

"Go ahead. Open the door," Spike threatened.

Looking dead into Spike's eyes, Clous said, "I can't. I don't know how."

"You'll do it if you don't want to die."

"I'm sorry, but I don't know how."

"You'd better find a way to open this door in the next twenty seconds, or you're dead."

"But please! I don't know how."

"Twelve seconds left."

"Shoot him. We will get in another way," Lovonous ordered.

"Wait, Wait!" screamed Clous.

"What do you have for me?" Lucian demanded.

Clous turned to answer when blood shot out of his mouth and a dagger point protruded from his chest. As his body fell, Spike's eyes came into view.

Lucian raged at Spike. "You fool! We needed that door open."

Spike was whipped around by an invisible force that knocked him to the ground. Lucian materialized on top of Spike, pounding the life out of him.

Lovonous quickly grabbed Lucian before he killed Spike. "Stop it, you two."

"He wasn't going to open that door anyway," Spike yelled as he patted himself down.

"We'll never know now," spat Lucian. "What do you propose we do now?"

"Quiet, we have company," Zererous said getting everyone's attention. He turned his x-ray vision on to see Lorous and Mars coming their way. "Hide that body."

Splitting up, they laid their trap. As Mars and Lorous came around the corner, Lovonous grabbed Mars and knocked Lorous out.

"Silence or you and your friend are dead," whispered Lovonous.

"What did you do to Lorous? Is she dead? Who are you?" Mars whined.

"Shut up and open this door." Lovonous spun Mars around to face the glowing chamber wall.

"I demand to know what you are doing here in this part of the castle."

Slapping Mars across the face, Lovonous again ordered Mars to open the door.

Mars looked up at Lovonous with blood flowing down his checks. Spitting out blood and some of his teeth, Mars yelled, "Please, don't hurt me."

Mars suddenly jumped back as Lucian popped up in front of him.

"Now, now. We won't hurt you but as for your freakish friend here…" Lucian's wicked teeth gleamed as he spoke, "that's another story."

"No, no. Don't hurt her." Looking down at Lorous, Mars could already see the blood pooling under her head. "I'll do it. Please get Lorous help."

"Get started," Lucian said.

Mars faced the door and waved his hands and mumbled an incantation. The door started to melt away leaving a gaping hole in the wall. Lucian pushed Mars inside and went in after him while the rest followed.

There before them was a beautiful ornate podium with

a chest sitting on it. Spike grabbed the chest. The power that emanated from the chest knocked Spike to the floor.

Lucian yelled, "Zererous check Spike." Turning, he grabbed Mars by the neck and started to squeeze. "What have you done?"

Zererous looked up at Lucian and shook his head. "I'm not getting a response."

Lucian continued to squeeze Mars even tighter, lifting him off the ground.

"Fix him!" Lucian growled.

Drool slipped out of Mar's lips as he said spoke his last, "I can't."

In the doorway, Lorous saw everything through a delirious state of mind. Half dead she turned and launched herself off the parapet.

"I'll get her," Lovonous said.

"No, leave her. Let's get that chest and get out of here," Lucian said.

Landing on the parapet, Morgan, Droll, Venous, and Ripkin spread out like pawns on a chess board. Morgan stepped forward and asked, "Did you get what we were looking for?"

Lucian's answer was a nasty grin. "How about you? Did you kill that Artie?"

"No, we couldn't even find him. He wasn't in any of the realms we looked," Morgan said.

"All is not lost," Lucian said. "We have the chest, but we can't move it. Anything that touches it is shocked with magical power."

"I've never seen or heard of magical power this strong except for our gifts. This must be made of the same star that the realms were.

"So, how are we going to move it?" Lucian said.

"Move aside, I'll get it," Ripkin said. He walked around the podium, squatted down, and shoved it enough to see if it would move. It did.

"Lovonous, you pick up the podium and the chest together, making sure not to move the chest," Ripkin commanded, casting his shield around him. "Now let's go."

Venous looked into the room and saw the low-hanging

tapestries and floor-length lace curtains. With one swift motion, Venous took in a deep breath and exhaled a cloud of fire against the tapestries. They quickly caught fire and spread up the wall toward the curtains. "Now let's go."

Moran yelled above the roaring blaze, "With this magical chest, Stous will turn the tide of war and get rid of that elf and his sidekicks."

As they flew away, Lorous watched from a neighboring parapet. She needed to report to Artie.

Chapter 10

-*Rhinosorous*-

Back on Aero, Leah said, "First, we need to get Qtrous."

Captain Christopher yelled, "Onward! I can see the triangle of stars dead ahead!"

Artie turned to the captain with a worried look. "I know these clouds you're heading into. They're very dangerous."

"But that's where the stars are leading us," Captain Christopher said.

"Yes," Artie continued, "that's true, but I'm giving you fair warning: you may want to take a longer way around. Going through these clouds isn't safe."

"No," Commander Leah said. "We've already wasted enough time. Qtrous might be in trouble, and we need to find him as soon as possible!"

Christopher turned to Leah. "Artie has never given us bad advice, and he knows the realms better than we do.

Maybe we should listen—"

"But, Captain, we must go this way. It's the fastest way!"

Christopher thought for a moment and then looked to Artie. The elf knew that Christopher couldn't say no to his sister. He smiled and bowed his head. "Let's do this," he shouted. "I see a rainbow ahead. Artie, which color of the rainbow do we take?"

"Each color is a different road," said the elf. "Each with different challenges."

"You choose the color, Captain," said Leah. "We'll follow you anywhere."

Christopher stared at the rainbow as Aero brought them closer and closer. "Aero," he commanded, "take the orange bow. We haven't tried that one yet."

The magic carpet changed course slightly, pointing itself directly toward the bow of orange light.

"Hang on!" yelled Artie just before the adventurers flew into the rainbow.

Aero slid into the orange light perfectly as a large blast of orange and gold light surrounded them. They rode along it without much shaking and stuttering.

"Hey, this isn't bad!" said Artie. "A lot smoother than that last green bow we rode."

"Yeah, great choice, Captain!" smiled Leah.

A few seconds later, their rainbow ride ended, and they found themselves in a new realm of Cloud Kingdom. They jumped down from Aero and began to look around.

"Wow!" exclaimed Leah, "Look over there." She pointed off in the distance with one hand shading her eyes. "The sun changes the way things look. And the colors, too. It looks like a forest of trees over there."

Artie looked in that direction and squinted. "That's because the rainbow took us to a different realm of the kingdom. Things take on a different form but so does the evil. We must be careful not to step into any traps set for us. As you already know, Stous is looking for us."

Just as Artie spoke those words, a cloud with a giant hand grabbed hold of Captain Christopher. With a single toss, the cloud threw him into a spiraling pit at the base of the clouds.

"Help me, you guys!" shouted Christopher as he fell

into the pit.

Leah ran toward the spiraling pit, but before she could help her brother, a camouflage hand grabbed her and threw her in the opposite direction. She tumbled through the air and flew through what looked to be a broken cloud.

As this happened, Artie dove back just in time to avoid the swatting of a giant tail. The creature—whatever it was—was huge! Artie tried to catch his breath, but the ground in front of him began growing and screeching. The sound was awful. A huge round head rose up from the cloud floor. The head was covered in spikes and fiery orange eyes glowed above snarling lips and curved fangs. Huge limbs followed as the creature grew completely out of the cloud floor. Its arms and legs were as thick as trees and built the same with extra appendages growing out like branches.

"What have you done with my friends?" shouted Artie.

"Get out of here, elf," the creature snarled. "They're mine now!"

Artie frowned and took a few steps backward. Then he raised his hands and brought them together with a thunderous clap. "Be gone, you ugly creature!" Artie yelled with a sly grin. Sparks flew from Artie's hands but died quickly. His hands fizzled, sizzled, and then nothing happened. Artie looked at his fingers, and his grin turned into a frown. Before he could react, the giant creature's spiked tail swooped around and hit Artie right on the rump. The elf flew head over heels through the air, traveling some distance before Aero caught him safely.

The creature laughed. "You have no powers here!"

Artie glared at the monster but knew better than to challenge it. "Aero," he said reluctantly, "get us out of here."

A moment later, Aero and Artie were a few mountaintops away from the monster.

"We have to find Captain Christopher and Commander Leah," Artie said to his flying carpet friend, "but how is the question. This looks very bad. I have no powers here. If ever we needed some help, it would be now."

Then Aero made a few gestures with its corners.

"Yes, I know. We need help."

Kneeling, Artie chanted an old incantation. He continued for a few moments when the sound of mountains rumbling filled the sky. The clouds rose above the mountain peaks and bright light filled the air. Artie looked up as a beautiful creature with huge, golden wings came floating down.

The creature had half the feline body of a wondrous mountain lion. The other half had majestic human qualities. Queen Ciella's feline head had exotic youthful skin and displayed her benevolent maternal wisdom. Her eyebrows flowed over her perfectly curved wide eyes. They showed understanding. Her pert nose and thin lips finished off the appearance of royalty. An astonishing wheat-colored mane encompassed her face and slightly covered gracefully pointy ears. Queen Ciella's Herculean chest had beautiful striations and her powerful biceps and triceps popped as she moved. She moved in one fluid motion. Her hands were human except for her fingers, which were tipped with retractable, talon-like claws. Flowing from the rounded muscular shoulders were regal wings of a golden-wheat color.

Chapter 11

–Queen Ciella–

"Ah, Queen Ciella, you shine so much brighter in your own realm that I didn't recognize you," Artie said.

"In the Orange Realm, the beauty is magnified by the brilliant and dazzling aura around it."

As Queen Ciella spoke, cat-like pixies flew about pollinating the precious flowers that created the angelic elixir that could only be found here in the Orange Realm.

"I see that you met Rhinosorous," the angelic creature said in a soothing voice."

"Yes," Artie replied, "unfortunately. Why can that creature rob me of my powers?"

"Oh, it wasn't he who robbed you of your powers. You still have them, but I'm the only one who can use magic in this realm."

Artie's eyebrows perked up. "All this time and I didn't know this. Queen Ciella, have you seen what happened to my friends Captain Christopher and Commander Leah?"

"Yes, I have," she answered. "But I must ask who these creatures are to you? They don't seem to have any magical powers, so why do they attract so much of your attention?"

"Well, they are my friends." Artie smiled. "They don't have magical powers, but they do have other qualities that I find admirable. They provide fellowship and camaraderie. They love one another. Commander Leah shows such loyalty to her captain. And she's full of so much gratitude towards Qtrous for saving her life that she's ready and willing to risk her own life to find him."

Queen Ciella smiled.

"Her brother, Captain Christopher, also shares those qualities. He also shows the courage and strength that it takes to lead and to do the right thing no matter what. They understand teamwork and cooperation. They know that there is no problem so big that it can't be solved by working together," Artie said.

"I agree with your assessment, but I see the hesitation in Christopher's eyes at times. Why is that?"

"Christopher has a hard time realizing that he has these gifts. So, fear creeps in and takes over."

"I agree that these two warrant closer watching," Queen Ciella pronounced. "I will gladly tell you what I know. Thank you for your assistance in our battle against Stous." She lifted an eyebrow and a sly grin crossed her face. "I heard you took a souvenir."

"Let's just say Stous's internal radar will be off." Artie chuckled and patted the pouch where he kept Stous's horn.

Chapter 12

-*Broken Clouds*-

"The one you call Leah," the queen continued, "was thrown through a broken cloud. Time and space were ripped inside the broken cloud so this could be a big problem. She could have come out the other side anywhere in Cloud Kingdom…at any time. Worse yet, a broken cloud can take apart a body and when it comes out the other side, the pieces may not go back together where they should."

"So, her arm could be where her leg is supposed to be," Artie gasped.

"Not only that. Different parts of Leah's body may be in different time zones altogether."

"My goodness and what happened to Captain Christopher?"

"Christopher was tossed into the spiraling pit that never stops. He could have been falling forever, but he outsmarted the Rhinosorous. As he was falling, Christopher took off his belt and hooked it into the top spiral. The belt unraveled with each turn, anchoring Christopher to the surface. I have already sent someone to collect him," Queen Ciella said.

On the other side of the Orange Realm, Rhinosorous stood face to face with an angry Egosorous.

"You fool," growled Egosorous. "You split them all up and now I need to gather them all together to capture them!"

"You paid me to separate them, so they'd be easier to capture," said Rhinosorous.

"Yes, but I didn't want you to destroy them! Broken clouds? Endless pits? You've made it ten times harder for me to capture them!"

Rhinosorous smiled shrewdly. "Sometimes I just can't control myself."

"I paid you well to get the job done, and you failed

me," Egosorous bellowed as he reached out his claw-like hand. "Now I'll have my payment back in full."

Rhinosorous growled, stomped his giant feet and wagged his tail, which resembled a rattlesnake ready to strike. "No one talks to me like that, let alone gets their payment back!"

Egosorous roared, standing on his alligator legs as he flamed on. He towered over the minion. He leaned down into Rhinosorous's face and snorted, "Give it up. Do not test me!"

Rhinosorous's eyes widened. Not many creatures were bigger than Rhinosorous, but he dared not challenge the fierce cloud creature in front of him. With no further hesitation, he returned the payment and felt relieved when Egosorous flew off to continue chasing his prey.

Rhinosorous snickered to himself. "At least it wasn't a total loss," he said. Opening two of the smaller hands on his arms, he examined the two golden amulets he'd taken from the outsiders.

"This is impossible," Artie muttered as he stumbled

through the clouds, pushing them aside to examine each as he walked. He was looking for the broken cloud that Leah had been tossed through, but the search seemed endless.

Off to the side, Aero stopped looking and shrugged.

"Well, keep looking. I'm sure this is where we were attacked, and—"

Artie froze as he spotted a broken piece of cloud with a strange material attached to it. He picked it up and examined it, trying to find a clue that would get Leah back. "I thought finding it would be the hard part. Now, I'm perplexed."

Suddenly, the air filled with bright light and the angelic Queen Ciella appeared before him.

"I see you've found it," she said, "and by now you've realized that this is a big mess to clean up."

Artie grimaced. "I need to save Leah, so let's not be so negative."

"Oh, I'm not negative. I'm truthful."

Artie sighed. "How about being helpful?"

Queen Ciella chuckled, then raised her graceful hand. "Sure," she said. "Step back."

Artie stepped away from the cloud fragments and watched as Queen Ciella waved her hands above the pieces. She chanted a short prayer and with a dazzling flash of color, the remnants of broken clouds melted together to form a large, oval mirror.

Chapter 13

-*Repaired*-

Artie peered into the mirror and saw himself, but instead of standing still, his reflection shook and looked frightened. "What is this?" he grumbled. "That's not me!" The elf waved his arms around, but his reflection remained the same.

"You're half right," smiled Queen Ciella. "The reflection is you, but it's who is inside. It's showing how you feel and right now you're scared for your friends, and you want them to be safe."

Artie shrugged. "Well, you're right about that. But how will this help get Leah back?"

"The mirror shows what's inside, not outside. Think about it."

Artie pondered for a few seconds before exclaiming, "And we need to know what's going on inside the broken cloud! Brilliant!"

Leah felt like she had broken into a million pieces. *What is going on inside me?* She tried to look down at her body but couldn't see herself and it frightened her. Suddenly, a familiar sight floated by: it was her torso with her bow and arrow floating behind it. "God, what's happened to me?" she screamed. *Keep calm, there must be an explanation for this. Christopher will find me. Or will he freeze up again?*

Queen Ciella smiled and gave him a nod. "Now get ready," she continued, "because a lot of fragmented information will come through the mirror quickly. Observe!"

Artie glued his eyes to the mirror as different images of Leah passed by. Parts of her floated by as if detached from her body. At one point, she was walking away from the mirror with her head turned to face them. In another, her head was gone entirely.

"This is a strange thing to watch," Artie said with a frown.

"Indeed," Queen Ciella said. "Now we must gather up everything here. They're all pieces of the whole image.

Leah's image. We need them all."

With that, Queen Ciella reached over to Artie and plucked a hair from his head. She swirled the hair around in her hands, chanting, while the hair slowly seemed to take on a life of its own. Queen Ciella opened her hands toward the mirror and the strand shot into the glass, swirling around in the clouds beyond.

"Now we wait," said Queen Ciella.

Artie nodded but turned quickly on his heels at an approaching sound behind them. "Captain Christopher!" he yelled, spotting the boy running toward them. Artie ran to Christopher and hugged him tightly.

"Good to see you too!" laughed the captain. "But where's Leah?"

"This is Queen Ciella, queen of this realm. She's helping us with a bit of bad news."

"I remember meeting her earlier." Christopher reached out to shake her hand but the queen only offered a deep bow.

"It's nice to see you free of the spiraling pit, Christopher," she smiled. "I can feel how nervous you are, so please let me explain."

Queen Ciella told Christopher every detail of where Leah had gone and what they'd done to rescue her.

"So, Artie's *hair* is out looking for her?" Christopher said with a puzzled look.

Queen Ciella grinned. "Something like that. I've touched it with my magic, so it can go into the broken cloud and gather all of the pieces that Leah left behind. In a few moments, it should have gathered all that there is."

With a sudden burst of light, a projection of Leah being thrown into the broken cloud flashed across the mirror. It showed her whole, then being broken into pieces, then whole again. The images repeated in an unending loop.

"What is happening?" yelled Christopher.

"Come with me," said Queen Ciella.

Gathering Artie, Aero, and Christopher together, she clapped her hands, and a bright flash surrounded them. In the next instant, they found themselves sitting around a beautiful ornate table.

"Please accept my heartfelt sorrow for your commander," Queen Ciella bowed. "She is now lost to the broken cloud world. She has passed the point of rescue, and no one has ever returned from this state."

Tears flowed immediately.

Captain Christopher jumped from his chair and shouted, "What are you talking about? I'm going back there, and I'm going in after her!"

Artie stood as well and raised his hands as if to calm Christopher. "Now wait a minute, don't just go off half crazy. We need a plan to get Leah back. Remember, it's teamwork that will win the day. So, sit back down and let's think about this."

Christopher tried to calm himself and sank back into his chair, telling himself that together they would work out a way to rescue his sister. But each time Artie or Christopher suggested an idea, Queen Ciella would explain why it wouldn't work. Christopher was frustrated and scared for his sister.

Chapter 14

–*Once More Into the Broken Clouds*–

Queen Ciella tried to swallow while her throat tightened as if she was chewing sand. Her foreboding grew with each moment. "I hesitate to mention it, but there might be one possibility. I have never tried it and there's very little chance that it will work."

"What is it?" Christopher yelled. "We have to try it, at least!"

Queen Ciella turned to Artie. "This will take your magic powers and mine," she told him.

"I thought you said my powers wouldn't work in this realm."

"That's true, but you won't be using your magic in my realm. You'll be using it in the broken cloud world."

"Wait. So you want us to go in there too?" Christopher said with a sideways glance at the queen.

"It's the only possible answer that I can see," Queen Ciella said. "But it can only work if Artie's magic works in that world and there's no guarantee that it will."

"We must take the chance," Christopher said.

"Christopher, are you willing to go through this?" Queen Ciella continued. "You must realize that if it doesn't work, you will be lost to the realm of the broken clouds, just like Leah."

Christopher stood up tall and erect. "Absolutely. Let's go."

Artie stood and slapped him on the back. "That's me boy!"

A clap of Queen Ciella's hands and they found themselves back at the mirror. The queen explained the details of her plan:

"After I place this enchantment on you, you will jump into the mirror of broken cloud. At the same time, Artie, you will need to summon up all the magic you can and direct it at Christopher. You must do this the moment

Christopher first breaks the plane of the clouds. No sooner, no later."

Artie nodded.

"Christopher, once this happens, you will start swirling counter-clockwise to slow down all the images of Leah and others who might be in there. These images will try to fool you and make you grab them. Be careful! However, once you see an image of Leah that is complete, you can grab hold of her and hug her tight. Then count to three, close your eyes, and say 'now.' You must make sure that she is complete when you hug her, or all is lost! If all works properly, you will both return."

Christopher couldn't bring himself to look in the mirror. He tried to clear his throat and found his tongue stuck to the roof of his mouth. His hands were sweating. "I've got it," said Christopher, secretly terrified. "I'm ready."

"Then prepare yourselves. Stand in front of the mirror."

They each took their place before the mirror, and Queen Ciella began waving her hands in a slow-moving arc. As her hands sped up, the air around them began to blur.

Christopher stared into the mirror with hands raised. Christopher yelled, "No way. I can't do this." Sweat poured off his body as he trembled and turned to meet Queen Ciella's gaze.

"It will be all right."

Christopher turned and ran right into Artie.

Artie shook his head. "No, don't do this."

Christopher took off at a fast pace, crying and mumbling, "I can't, I can't." His body gave out and he fell forward. Christopher couldn't believe he was such a coward. Even if he could summon up the courage now to take on the mission, nothing would be the same. No one would respect him anymore, let alone talk to him or want to be with him. Bowing his head, he wept. He jumped when something touched him and he turned to see Artie sit down next to him and put his arm around the young adventurer.

Artie spoke in a soft, comforting voice. "It's okay, Christopher; it's okay. Please look at me."

Lifting his head, the tears rolled down his cheeks. Christopher tried to settle his rapid breathing in short gasps.

"Tell me what's wrong."

"Sometimes when I stop to think about the danger, my mind takes over and I can't follow through to do the right thing."

"That's fear, and it can be crippling. It happens to everyone; most people never get past it. Then some people do get past it and live a freer life because of it."

"How do they get past that fear?"

"There are many ways. Usually, it's because they think with their heart and not their mind. You'll have to dig deep and find the reason that works for you."

"I know I do, but it seems so hard when I think about it."

"I have seen you go past that fear on and off since you have been here in Cloud Kingdom. How did you feel when you took off the dragon's head to save me?"

"I felt like I had done something good and it felt good. But you and Leah were there with me."

"This is no different! Every time fear strikes, remember

what's on the other side. The reward is always worth the risk in those cases. As you already know, this brings freedom."

Standing, Artie brushed himself off and helped Christopher up. "Take your time and decide if you want to carry on with this mission. There'll be no judgment either way. Just remember what the stakes are—Leah."

"I'm done thinking about this. I'm sorry; let's do this. If I falter, just push me through!"

"Let's go, then," Artie said.

They stood in front of the mirror again.

Christopher nodded his head. "Let's do this."

"Get ready to jump as soon as I cast my enchantment," Queen Ciella said. "Now!"

With a snap of magical energy, the enchantment fired from Queen Ciella's hands and connected with Christopher just as his feet left the ground. In the following instant, two things happened simultaneously. Artie cast a stream of rainbow colors and stardust toward the mirror and a cloud explosion ripped into the mirror. Artie did not know if his powers surrounded Christopher in time. The colorful glow just disintegrated as he crossed the glass.

Beyond the glass, Christopher started spinning just as he had been told he would. As he rotated counterclockwise, he saw dozens of different images of Leah spinning around him. Some were just pieces of his sister, and some were so small Christopher couldn't even be sure they were part of her. He reached out toward an image of Leah's face but pulled his hands back when he remembered that he needed a complete image. The copy gave a frightening cackle as Christopher backed away and he forced himself to concentrate on the remaining images.

A moment later, Christopher spotted two identical images of Leah. They looked complete, but it was impossible to tell which one was truly her—mind, body, and soul. Christopher's eyes darted back and forth from one Leah to the next. He had no idea which image to grab until one gave him a sly look and mouthed, "Oh, man, grab me!"

Christopher quickly grabbed that version of Leah, hugged her tightly, and blinked. Exploding clouds and a rushing wind swirled around them, tossing them every which direction within the broken cloud world. Outside, beyond the glass, Artie and Queen Ciella waited anxiously. Suddenly, a flash of color and swirling clouds filled the mirror.

"I think I see them!" shouted Artie, but before he could be sure, the mirror went dark.

Back in the lower Orange Realm, Rhinosorous was looking over the strange items he'd stolen from the outsiders. "What are these things, and how do they work?" he mumbled to himself as his many hands twirled, rubbed, and shook them. His hands flipped the two gold pieces and fumbled with them randomly. Finally, he decided to push the two pieces together. When he did, his entire body began to shake and rumble. Rhinosorous shut his eyes to the shock of raw energy that shot through him. He opened his eyes an instant later and found himself somewhere far from the Orange Realm. Somewhere full of angry dark clouds and ferocious beasts.

"Stratocloudous!" he said, panic tinting his voice. "But…how…"

Rhinosorous turned his massive spiked head and saw something even less welcoming: Egosorous looming over him with his lips stretched into a wicked grin.

"Well, well," Egosorous hissed. "Isn't this a lucky break? I've wanted to talk to you more about how many problems you've caused me." Egosorous snickered so loudly it shook the ground.

Nearby, Qtrous watched it all through half-swollen eyes.

Chapter 15

–A Loss–

Artie paced back and forth in front of a large mirror that seemed to be made of swirling clouds. The queen watched him with concern in her eyes.

"I must get back to Cloud City," Artie said. "It's been hours and we still haven't seen or heard from Captain Christopher and Commander Leah." Artie hung his head and shook it. "I know. I fear the worst. I will leave a sentry."

The queen interrupted. "What is your carpet trying to tell you?"

The carpet signed something with his tassels.

"He says he's felt something in the Rainbow Causeway…an unusual presence."

"Could it be Leah and Christopher?" Artie looked at Aero and frowned as the magic carpet shrugged. "He doesn't know," said the elf, "but we must find out."

Deep in the black heart of Stratocloudous, the wicked Egosorous loomed over Rhinosorous and fumed with anger. "You've got a lot of explaining to do, Rhinosorous," the giant monster spat. "Like for starters, I want to know how you got here and what it is that you're hiding between your greedy little fingers."

Rhinosorous looked frightened and confused. "I don't know how I got here," he stammered. "I was just trying to put these two pieces of jewelry together… and then I appeared here."

"There's more to it than that," Egosorous cut in, "so tell me. I am losing my patience with the likes of you."

"I don't know anything else! Do you think if I knew how this worked, I'd bring myself back here? The last thing I wanted to see was *you*. I was better off with those lousy kids."

Egosorous's eyebrows shot up at that remark, and he bared his sharp teeth. He looked as if he was about to pounce when a booming voice interrupted.

"Shut up, the both of you," thundered Stous, the most

feared beast in Stratocloudous. "Bring me those trinkets."

Rhinosorous stepped timidly toward Stous, nearly leaping away when Stous snatched the two pieces from his wrinkly, thick-skinned hand. Stous tilted his massive head, using the eye that Qtrous hadn't robbed him of to examine the fragments. Holding the amulets out by their chains, he shouted toward Rhinosorous. "Where did these come from?"

Rhinosorous lowered his head and snorted, a sign that Stous knew well enough to mean that the creature was about to lie. "We found them in the Yellow Realm," Rhinosorous grunted.

"Funny," Stous snarled, again showing his pointed teeth. "I thought you just came from the Orange Realm..." Stous stared down Rhinosorous.

The shadow of Egosorous could be seen on the wall and looked as if it were dancing. Egosorous was doing anything but. His head hung low and his feet were quietly shuffling him out of sight. If Stous questioned him about the kids, Rhinosorous would speak up and tell of Egosorous's part in the kids going missing. He had to get out.

Spiraling downward and landing in the backyard, Chris looked at Leah. "Oh man, that was such a close call. I didn't know if we'd make it back, let alone find you. Are you okay, Leah?"

"Yes, I think so," she said with a strained voice. "What the heck has been going on? What happened to me? I feel like I was in a hundred different places at the same time."

"You probably were."

Leah gave him a questioning look.

"I'll tell you later."

"It was brave of you to come after me," said Leah, picking herself up from the grass.

Christopher lowered his head and mumbled a thank you. He remembered what he had done in front of the mirror. Their backyard was quiet, and it was dark outside.

"Thank you, Chris." Leah put out her hand and helped her brother up from the ground. "What would I do without my Commander?"

He smiled, brushing grass from his clothes. "Let's

get back upstairs before the dogs realize we're out here," whispered Christopher, "and wake up the whole neighborhood."

The siblings made their way into the house quietly, taking the back stairs all the way up to their bedrooms. Leah veered off into Christopher's room to finish their conversation. Once settled in with the door shut behind them, they heard a voice.

"Children, why aren't you asleep yet? Get to bed," Mother yelled.

"Sorry, okay," they called out in unison.

"Okay, tell me what happened," Leah pleaded.

"I'll explain later. We should let Artie and Queen Ciella know that we're all right. I'm sure they're worried."

"Okay," Leah said. "Let's do that right now. The amulets can get us back to them right away."

Christopher reached under his shirt for his amulet, but found nothing. "Oh no," he gasped, "I can't believe this! I lost my amulet!"

Leah frowned. "What could have happened to it? What are you going to do?"

"It must have fallen off when I jumped in the mirror," Chris sighed. "Get your half out and see if maybe it can help us find mine!"

Leah reached up to her neck and nearly jumped. Chris watched her eyes turn red and swell with tears.

"Mine's gone too," she whispered, dropping her hand back to her lap.

"This isn't good," said Chris. "And it's getting too late for us to do anything about it."

Leah yawned as if prompted by the remark. "But we need to get those amulets back."

"We need rest," said Chris. "Once we get some sleep, we can tackle that adventure."

Chapter 16

-Bullies-

The nighttime hours passed, and at dawn, the sun shone brilliantly through Chris and Leah's bedroom windows. Leah rolled over in her snug, warm bed and blinked her eyes open to the sunrise. Jumping out of bed to wake Christopher, she opened his bedroom door only to find him already up and ready, pacing back and forth in the kitchen, wondering what his dad was going to say about the bullies.

Their mother's voice drifted down the hall. "It's time for school! Let's get going!"

"Morning, Son," said Christopher's father as he walked into the kitchen.

Gulping, Chris replied, "Morning, Dad."

"Well, Son, I've thought about what you said last night. I talked to your mother, and we both think you should go to a military school. They have a better educational program that will meet your accelerated learning, which is going so well. I'm proud of you in those areas. Also, they can help build character, so you will be ready when it's your time to serve your country."

Looking up at his dad, Christopher felt like someone had punched him in the gut. With all the air out of his lungs, he started to heave. His face turned red and tears rolled down his cheeks. He gasped. Sucking air back into his lungs, he turned and ran into the bathroom. Sitting on the floor, he cried silently. Opening the door, Christopher yelled, "Dad, you can't do this to me. Please don't. It only happened once; I promise it won't happen again and I promise I'll have my stuff back by tomorrow. Please, please!"

"Son, I know that right now this sounds like the end of the world. But I assure you that it's not. We'll talk more about it tonight. Come, say good-bye. I have to get to the base."

Leah snapped into action, grabbed a pack of fruit snacks, and ran to the bus stop. Christopher looked like he'd been through the war as he shuffled down to meet his sister.

"What was Dad talking to you about?"

"I can't talk about it now. I'll tell you later."

"I heard him say something about military school."

"Dad doesn't like it when I'm not strong. When he found out that a girl took something from me, he thought I lost my honor and wants to send me to military school. The two sat quietly and watched as the usual clowns acted up. The bullies seemed to be out in full force and one was picking on the new kid at school, Ben. Christopher was ready to stand up and say something when Leah put her hand on his shoulder and pushed him back in his seat.

Christopher looked up in shock as Leah faced the bully. In a booming voice, she told him: "Stop it right now, and sit down!"

The bus instantly turned silent. It had never been quieter. Everyone sat still, in shock, until the bus pulled into the school parking lot.

When the bully, Thomas, got off first he waited for Ben to pass and whispered," I'll get you later."

Leah overheard Thomas's threat. "Not on my watch, you bully!"

He looked back at her and snarled. Leah and Christopher followed Ben to safety.

"What was that all about?" Christopher asked her.

"We all know how you are when it comes to conflict."

"What are you talking about?"

"Let's just say that the word 'freeze' comes to mind," Leah said and raced off.

Christopher lowered his head. *Does she know that I froze by the mirror? How? Did Artie tell her? Or Queen Ciella?*

Christopher and Leah both went through the day thinking of Queen Ciella and Artie. How could they get back to Cloud Kingdom? How could they let their friends know they were okay? Their teachers' voices seemed to drone on and on. Whole sentences sounded like single words and the day seemed to drag on for what seemed like hours.

Christopher saw Leah ahead of him when school let out and yelled at her. She turned and acknowledged him for a moment, then kept walking. Christopher caught up with her at the west wing exit, and they walked out of school together so they could talk about their return to Cloud Kingdom.

Their planning was cut short when they heard a ruckus.

"Sissy!" one of the bullies yelled at Ben. "You're worse than a girl!"

Another bully laughed. "He'd be one ugly girl."

The first bully reached out and shoved Ben. Before Chris and Leah could reach the group, another bully behind Ben tripped him, sending him flying with a grunt onto his back.

Christopher scowled and turned to Leah. "I'll meet you at the bus. I got this." He stepped off toward the growing crowd.

"Oh, no you don't," said Leah, straightening her back and running to catch up with him. "I started this, so back off. I got this." Leah's face was tight and stern, ready to take on all comers.

As brother and sister reached the crowd, the chanting of mean names and insults grew louder. It seemed to be coming from everywhere as if the bullies had inspired half the school to turn against the new kid.

Leah slid through the crowd, ignoring their mean remarks, and walked directly to Thomas, the lead bully. Thomas was startled when Leah put her arm around him and then leaned over to whisper something in his ear. The bully stared blankly for a second, shook his head, and walked away. The crowd grew quieter and even Christopher looked shocked to see Thomas moving out of the group and away from Ben.

"Where are you going?" the other bullies called after him.

It took only seconds for the other bullies to take off on Thomas' heels and the rest of the crowd to start fading away.

"You should mind your own business," said Ben.

Leah realized he was talking to her. She was a bit surprised, but she just looked at Ben and smiled.

As the new kid walked away, Christopher stepped beside Leah and whispered, "That was crazy! Leah, what did you think you were doing?" Christopher asked her in a stern voice.

"I told you I had this, and besides, I don't hesitate when I make a decision."

Christopher mumbled something as he started to walk away, then stopped and turned to Leah. "What did you say to Thomas to make him stop dead like that?"

Leah smiled. "I told him I didn't think he would like it if everyone knew that at his last school, he was always the one getting picked on. And that he cried all the way home to his mommy and daddy."

"Wow, that would sure hurt his reputation."

Leah nodded. As they walked off toward the bus, her brother said, "Hey, what do you make of Ben telling you to mind your own business? I bet he hated being helped by a girl."

"I know, but that's stupid. For the moment, he was the center of attention and it made him feel important, even if it was negative attention. He could have gone the other way and said thank you. He would have learned that by respecting yourself you become important, not only to yourself but to others around you."

Christopher nodded and chuckled.

They both giggled as they continued toward the bus for the ride home.

As they headed toward the bus, Leah's girlfriends called after her. She looked at Christopher and said, "I'll meet you at the bus stop."

"Okay. See ya." Around the corner in the schoolyard, he turned right into the Tara twins, Eddie and Liz, with their friend Jeffery and a few more of their cronies.

"Well, well, look who we have here. Got any new cool stuff for me?" the girl who took his shiny racecar asked.

Christopher froze in his tracks. His mind raced and his veins pulsated through his skin as his heartbeat got louder and his mouth went dry. His stomach felt like he had been on the spider ride in a carnival. The laughing and taunting became louder and faster the closer they got to him.

Christopher managed to get in front of the tall boy, who had ripped his backpack. He lifted his hands up and started to ask for his lead pencil back. However, nothing came out of his mouth but dry air. The whole group now began to laugh and taunt him. Frozen, he looked at the eyes looking at him. Eyes that seemed to say, "You are worthless! Where is your honor?"

Petrified, tears welled up in Christopher's eyes. As the first tear ripped out from behind his eyelid, Christopher turned and broke through all the kids and ran off. The laughter was nearly deafening in his ears. A voice found its way into his consciousness. 'Where is your honor, boy?' Slowing to a stop, he bent over heaving and gulping for air. As the air slowly came back, he could hear his own heart beat louder and louder. The cadence was rough at first. It didn't match the new voice in his head.

Taking deeper breaths and calming himself, he heard the voice beat to a new cadence, and it repeated over and over, 'This won't be easy, but you can do it. You have always been able to do this; you have the power.' Shaking his head and closing his eyes tight, Christopher could see Artie, the Elf, telling him, 'You got this.' Then he saw his sister standing there. 'We all know that you froze.' Lifting his head, he straightened himself up to full height. He said to himself, I'm *in no mood for this! Not today.*

With an uncompromising look, Christopher marched back to the huddle of bullies and stared at them as one yelled, "He's back." The older boy whipped around to see Christopher walking straight toward him.

The older boy backed up a step as he looked into Christopher's eyes and saw no tears, no fear, just pure determination.

When Christopher reached his target, he stretched out a hand and said, "Give it up. I want all my stuff back now!"

The older boy looked around to make sure no one could see his nervous grin. He stuttered, "What are you going to do about it?"

Christopher gritted his teeth and said, "Whatever it takes! How about you? What are you willing to do?"

Before the kid could answer, the teacher came around the corner.

"Break it up; we will not tolerate any fighting here on the school premises."

Christopher, full of adrenaline, turned and walked back to the bus station. All he could hear was, "You're going to have to go to military school." Now that he had lost the opportunity to get his stuff back that day, it was a done deal.

PART

 # THREE

"Whatever journey you choose in life,
may it be joyous, happy, and free."

PART

THREE

Whatever journey you choose in life
may it be joyous, happy and free.

TABLE OF CONTENTS

—PART THREE—

Chapter 1

-*Sad Reward*-

Tossing their backpacks down in the mudroom, Chris and Leah rushed to the kitchen to grab snacks from the pantry.

"How was school, kids? Did you have a good day?" Their Mom joined them in the kitchen and examined their faces.

Christopher and Leah tried to hide any concern about Artie and their other friends in Cloud Kingdom.

"You know you can't fool me," said their mom. "What's going on?"

Leah's eyes widened, and she looked at her brother. Christopher hunched his shoulders and ducked his head.

"Come on you two! What gives?"

"Well," said Leah, "there were some bullies on the bus."

"Yeah!" interrupted Christopher. "And Leah shut them up!"

Mom looked concerned for a moment, then smiled. "Time to get your homework done while I cook dinner. And…for doing such a good deed today, Leah gets to pick out dessert. What kind of ice cream would you like?"

"Peanut butter chocolate," said Leah without hesitation.

Mother nodded, and Leah and Christopher headed out of the kitchen to finish their homework. As they walked upstairs, Leah whispered to her brother, "Imagine what reward I would get if she found out about me helping Qtrous in Cloud Kingdom."

"A monster almost ate you, so you'd either get a lifetime supply of ice cream, or you'd be grounded until you're 40!"

Christopher and Leah finished their homework early, watching the rain beat down on the blistered windowpanes. They talked for a while about how to return to Cloud Kingdom without their amulet, but couldn't come up with an answer.

Frustrated, Chris rolled off the bed. "I'm going to go play my video game."

"Oh, no you're not!" said Leah. "We have to figure this out."

Christopher walked toward the door against his sister's protests but was stopped suddenly by the sun flashing brightly through the window. He blinked and squinted out the window, his narrowed eyes falling on the most astounding rainbow he'd ever seen. The rainbow itself was huge, and each color appeared as an unusually broad band of light.

"Did you hear that?" said Leah, turning toward her brother.

"No," he shrugged. "Let me go play. I'm going to see if my friend Dylan from Virginia is on his game."

Leah jumped up and grabbed Chris by the arm. "No way!" she said. "Don't you hear what I'm hearing?"

"You're nuts, girl. I just want to be left alone for a bit to play my game."

Leah let go of her brother's arm and sighed. "You

know," she grumbled, "you've been a grumpy old pudge since we lost those amulets."

Christopher ignored the remark and stomped off, thinking about how he was going to prove he was no coward. *That teacher had to show up just when I had a shot at getting my stuff back. Then dad would have to think twice about me being a coward or sending me to military school.*

Leah heard him start the video game in the next room.

Chapter 2

- A New Realm -

Leah huffed and turned her head to the window. She spotted the enormous rainbow and gasped; it was positively huge, and it looked like it might even be growing. It became wider and the strange humming noise in her ears became louder.

"How can he not hear that?"

Leah blinked and stared at the rainbow. It was growing larger or at least part of it was. Right before her eyes, the blue bow of the rainbow started expanding, getting larger by the second, and pushing its way closer to the window. Seconds later, the bow of blue light forced its way into the window of Leah's room and glided to a stop right at her feet.

"Chris!" she yelled, "Get in here!"

"Busy!" his voice came back from his room.

"No," yelled sister as she stepped onto the strip of blue light. "It's time to go back! Hurry!"

Just as the words left her mouth, the rainbow began to pull her toward the sky. The whole world started to glow bright blue. She could barely make out Christopher rushing around the corner, swinging on the doorframe and coming to a sudden stop. He stared at her in complete shock, his mouth open as he stared at the big blue strip of light. He jumped toward the rainbow but landed flat on his face. The room was empty—no blue light, no Leah.

"Leah!" Chris yelled into the air. "Leah, come back!"

As Chris stared at the empty room, worry filled him. *With all the craziness that happened in Cloud Kingdom, how will I look out for her being stuck down here.* He'd all but given up hope when the room flashed with dazzling light and color. A cloud of stardust drifted through the air, and when Christopher blinked away the colors in his eyes, he saw Leah standing in the middle.

"Christopher!" she yelled. "The rainbow showed me Artie and Queen Ciella! It even showed me where to find Qtrous!"

Christopher jumped to his feet and grabbed Leah by the arm. "Where did you go?" he yelled. "You left me here, and I was so worried!"

"I was on the blue bow of the rainbow," she said, waving her hand. "It's all good. You taught me how to be strong. Besides, it wasn't my fault you were too slow to jump on the rainbow."

Christopher stared at her grimly.

"Anyway," continued Leah, "I saw Artie and Queen Ciella standing at the mirror but I couldn't talk to them. I guess in the blue rainbow you can see and hear things, but you can't touch them or talk to anyone."

"You said you saw Qtrous, too?"

"Yes. He got out of that dungeon that Stous had him in, but he's still a prisoner on Stratocloudous."

"So, we still need to get up there and help him escape?"

"Yup," added Leah, "before Stous or his minions find him. And speaking of Stous, I saw him too. He has our amulets."

"Oh no," Christopher said, jumping to his feet. "We can't let him have our amulets! We need to get them back and soon." Christopher paused for a moment, then huffed, "Not that we know how to get back."

Leah jumped up and smiled, "I know how! I overheard

Artie and Queen Ciella talking about us, and he said that as long as we remember to call on Elephantous, we can get back!"

"Wow," said Christopher, "I can't believe I didn't think of that."

"Oh, you would have eventually," Leah insisted.

Christopher chuckled and shrugged. "Maybe. But before we go, there's something else we need to take care of."

Chapter 3

– Plan,

Betrayal or Friend–

"We have to make sure that Ben is safe," Chris said.

"I don't know," said Leah. "I think we need to go now. There's no time to waste!"

"Calm down, sis. It's not wasting time. He needs our help. Besides, I think I can take care of this pretty fast."

"What have you got planned, Chris?"

"Well, we already proved that the ringleader of these bullies is just as scared as Ben. The only difference is that he takes it out on other kids. He's got a real mean streak."

"I'll say," added Leah.

"But I don't think it's his fault."

"How can it not be his fault? I didn't see anyone else

stirring up trouble."

"Not right in front of us," said Christopher, "but I know more about Thomas than you think. I know he has an older brother who picks on him all the time. I've seen it."

"So, bullying is all this poor kid knows? I knew he was bullied but not by his own family." Leah frowned. "But what can you do about that? Remember, we have to take care of this fast and get back to Artie."

"I know. But this is important too. Tomorrow we'll try to help talk everyone through this problem. I'll talk with Thomas. You talk to Ben."

"I'm listening," said Leah, crossing her arms impatiently. "But this time you can't hesitate as you did at the mirror."

Christopher's head shot up and he looked at Leah with surprise. He could barely spit the words out. "I know, I know, Leah. I'm so sorry I ran away. My mind thinks and sees things so fast that sometimes it overrides my actions. I don't know who told you but I'm sorry. I would never have left you there."

"Well, no one told me. I saw you run away from the mirror."

Hearing this, Christopher hung his head, closed his eyes, and relived those awful moments. Raising his head, the shame on his face told the story. He looked into his sister's eyes. "Not one of my finest moments. I promise it won't happen again."

"Okay, so what's your plan?" Leah grumbled.

"You need to meet Ben after one of his classes and ask him to help you in the boiler room. When he asks why you need help, just tell him you need to take some stuff from the art room down there for storage."

"And what are you going to do?"

"I'm going to tell Thomas I know a secret shortcut under the school to the gym. I'll take him down to the boiler room. Once they're both in the room, the door will automatically shut behind them and lock. They'll need a code to open it from the inside."

"They'll be stuck in there together? Are you sure that's a good idea?"

"If they want to get out, they'll have to work together.

Nothing makes people get along like needing each other to get out of a jam!"

"Cool," Leah said as she headed downstairs. "I'm hungry. Let's get some food."

Dad walked in from work with a look of concern on his face.

"What's wrong?" said Mom.

"The Navy has changed its mind on when we are moving." Dad whispered. "They are sending me on deployment for six months to a year. We'll need to tell the kids after dinner."

"You know that this is the third time they have changed their minds on what to do with your unit. It's getting old. Don't they have families?"

He hugged her and whispered, "It will be all right."

"Let's wait 'til tomorrow before we tell them."

"All right."

The next day, Leah and Chris set about their plan. Leah caught up with Ben in the halls after class, and Christopher made sure Thomas headed down to the basement about the same time.

A few minutes after setting them on their paths, Leah and Christopher went down to the dark corridors beneath the school. On tiptoe, they approached the boiler room just in time to see the door slam shut behind Thomas with a loud click.

"It worked!" whispered Christopher, and he and his sister both dashed for the door.

Kneeling, they peered into the boiler room through the slats of a vent in the door. They could see the shadows of the boiler's flames dancing on each other's face and feel the dry heat.

"You let the door close!" Ben yelled.

"Yeah, so?" said Thomas. "Why are you down here anyway?"

Fear pushed Ben into action. He jumped on the bully. Before Thomas could react, Ben was sitting on top of him.

"Ow!" the bully groaned, "get off me!"

"If I get off you, will you leave me alone? We can be friends, or not, but just promise you're going to stop bothering me!"

"Whatever, man," gasped Thomas. "Just get off me!"

Ben jumped up and Thomas stood up. They stared at each other, the fire from the boiler reflecting in their eyes. Thomas raised his hand and Ben quickly, but awkwardly, brought up both of his fists. "I knew I couldn't trust you. You're a bully."

"Chill, man," said Thomas as he extended his hand to shake with Ben.

Ben looked into Thomas's eyes, then at his hand before grabbing it to shake.

"It's too hot to fight in here anyway," grinned Thomas.

Ben looked a bit worried until the bully slapped him on the back and laughed.

"Let's get out of here, alright?" Thomas suggested.

"The door's locked."

"I figured as much," said Thomas, craning his neck to look around the room. He noticed a small stream of light coming from near the ceiling. "That's the cellar door!"

Ben ran to the wall and looked up. "And there's no lock on it. But it's high up there. I can't reach it. By the way, why did you choose me to pick on?"

"You always walked with your head down and looked weak—you looked frightened, like you didn't belong."

"I'll have to change that."

"At least walk with your head up and look at people or greet them."

"How do you know these things?"

"I'll tell you a secret, but you got to promise never to tell a soul. Okay?"

Worriedly, Ben nodded.

Thomas anxiously looked about for a way to reach the cellar door as he mumbled, "My brother Cliff always picks on me and I'm always afraid to be near him. Come to think of it, my dad is the same. Now let's get out of here."

Thomas raised an arm in the air and stood on his toes. "Yeah, I can't reach it either," he said and then got down on one knee. "Here, step into my hands."

"What?"

"Stand on my hands, and I'll lift you up there."

Ben climbed onto Thomas's interlocked fingers and, with a grunt, the larger boy hoisted him a good four feet into the air. Ben reached up and easily pushed one side of the cellar door aside. Bright sunlight exploded into the room so suddenly that Ben almost fell over.

"Whoa there!" said Thomas, shaking to keep his balance. "Grab the ledge and pull yourself up. Quick!"

Ben pulled himself up to the outside and turned around. Hanging his arms down into the boiler room, he gestured for Thomas to grab hold.

"They're out!" whispered Leah as she squinted through the slats of the vent.

"Let's go," said Chris. "We'll meet them outside."

Brother and sister jumped to their feet and ran for the exit.

As Chris and Leah approached the cellar door, they saw Thomas and Ben brushing themselves off. Everything seemed to be going well until they spotted another group of older kids moving in their direction.

"Hey, Thomas!" one of the kids yelled. Scared witless, both boys whipped around only to see another new gang. "Is that the little creep you were telling us about?"

Chris held out his arm and stopped Leah in her tracks. "Let's see what happens," he whispered. They watched as Thomas gave Ben a long, examining look. It was as if the bully realized how much he and his former victim had in common.

"Nah," said Thomas. "He's my friend."

"Sure," laughed the other boy. "Sure, he is."

"I'm telling you he is, Cliff," Thomas said again, this time with a scowl.

Worry washed over Ben's face as the exchange continued. He looked at Thomas with pale cheeks and asked, "Do you know these guys?"

"Yeah," said Thomas. "This is Cliff, my big brother."

Ben nearly leaped out of his shoes as he stepped away from Thomas. "What?!" he choked, "So this was a trap?"

"No," said Thomas, "Trust me. I had no idea he'd be here. Let's just get out of here. You'll be all right. Cliff can't afford to start another fight. One more and the school will expel him."

Cliff laughed. "Your friend sure is jumpy."

"But he is my friend, so back off," Thomas yelled.

Chapter 4

- *The Return* -

Christopher and Leah had kept their distance throughout the whole encounter, but they could see Ben smiling as he and Thomas walked away together. Chris nearly cheered when the former bully put his arm around Ben's shoulder and the two boys started laughing together like old friends.

"Oh, man!" said Leah, "That worked perfectly!"

Christopher smiled and tapped the side of his head to suggest it was all brain power then gave his sister a high five and a fist bump. "Alright, let's get home so we can get to work on our other mission."

Hopping on the school bus, they began drawing up a plan to call Elephantous. Once at home, they continued discussing it in their rooms until their parents called for them to come down. "We're going out for dinner tonight. First, we need to tell you guys something, so go sit down at the dinner table."

"What is it, Dad?" Leah said.

"The Navy has changed its mind, and we won't be moving this year."

"I already contacted the school for both of you, so they expect you this coming week," Mom said.

"Christopher, remember we discussed you attending a military school?"

"Yes, Dad."

"That might have to wait till I get back," Dad said.

Christopher tried to hide his relief as he relaxed back in his chair.

"The Navy is deploying me for six months to a year. Christopher, I will see if I can transfer you to the school on base. Okay, go get in the car. Time for dinner."

Christopher's relief was short-lived as his father's words settled in his brain. Tremors started inside his stomach, climbed straight up to his heart, and manifested into tears.

After dinner when they were going back upstairs, Leah said to Christopher, "I won't let Dad send you to military school."

"I don't want to talk about it now."

"Okay."

"Come on," Christopher said and pulled out his pouch of magic dust.

Leah grabbed the white towel out of the linen closet and rushed to her brother's side, tossing the towel on the floor between them. Chris pulled a handful of magic dust from the pouch and prepared to sprinkle it on the towel. He hesitated for a moment, then moved his hand closer to Leah's face with a grin.

His sister understood and blew the sparkling powder from his palm. The cloud of dust drifted onto the towel and the air filled with a string of *snaps, sizzles,* and *pops.*

They giggled in delight. "Oh man, here we go again!"

The towel started to move and wiggle this way and that. A moment later, it began to take on the shape of a fluffy, white elephant. Elephantous took form and swooped around the room. Leah and Christopher gave him a wink. He smiled at them and they felt themselves getting smaller as the room grew around them. A second later, Elephantous wrapped the adventurers up in his trunk, tossed them onto his back, and carried them out the window.

The floor shone under Kolya's feet where his robe dragged on the floor. Kolya stopped pacing and stood hunched backed and addressed the assembly.

"As you know, our young, our most precious gift and resource are being captured or killed. We must find out how and why! Like yours, my realm is not a realm of war. We must seek outside help. I nominate one of our younger elders to seek out the Council. Do we agree on this course of action?"

Unanimously, the elders raised their arms in the air and chanted, "The Council!"

"Okay, who do we send?"

Each elder looked at each other then stepped forward.

Kolya smiled. "For now, one pair will do."

As the elders circled to make their choice, Kolya chanted a prayer asking for wisdom. Paola from the realm of Ancient Scrolls and Oda from Purple Paradise stepped forward. Paola had a lovely long, slender body, and her mane flowed down her slightly arched back. Her tail was perfect in proportion to her body. Speed, stealth, and wisdom were her most significant attributes. Oda was tall with a muscular torso and limbs that rippled with defined muscular tone. Strength, speed, lightning thought processes, and magical enchantments were his greatest attributes. They complemented each other in looks, power, beauty, and deception.

"A lot has happened since our last couple of scrimmages with Stous's minions over the souls and dreams of our youth, but it's been quiet around here lately," Artie explained to Queen Ciella.

Lord Mason ripped through a porthole. "Excuse the instantaneous entrance. I have a message from Elder Kolya. Please expect two of our emissaries with a dire plea."

As he spoke, the Rainbow Causeway dropped off two delegates from the realms. Bowing low to Queen Ciella, and pledging themselves to Artie, the introductions began.

"Thank you, Lord Mason, Queen Ciella, and Artie for seeing us. My name is Oda, and my partner is Paola. We have just come from an emergency meeting of the elders," Oda said.

"Pray tell, what is going on that we need an emergency meeting of the Council?" Queen Ciella said.

Paola's long, reddish mane covered the wrinkles on her face as she explained, "We think the Evil Eight has systematically hit each realm on the outskirts of the territories. Hitting the young creatures as they slept, they stole their souls and dreams and replaced them with nightmares."

"There are reports from people who have seen a frozen shadowed look upon their faces," said Oda. "They say they were hellish to gaze upon. We believe the Evil Eight caged them in Tundrasorous. Parents everywhere are complaining of the disappearance of their young."

Paola picked up again. "Constables could not figure this out. They brought their problems to the Elders. The elders of all the realms called for a special meeting. Out of all the propositions shouted out, none were agreed on except to seek out the Council."

Elephantous flew Leah and Chris skyward and a split second later they found themselves landing softly on a pile of clouds. In the distance, Elephantous glided off until he was little more than a speck.

"Where are we?" asked Commander Leah.

Christopher looked around, noticing familiar shapes and colors in the clouds.

"I hate to say this," he grumbled, "but this looks like Stratocloudous."

"I think Elephantous brought us to the amulets," deduced Leah. "Why else would he bring us to this awful place?"

"I don't know, but I want to get out of here as fast as possible, so we'd better start looking."

Stous watched as the two children landed on the dark clouds in the distance. He smiled a wicked grin, showing rows of jagged teeth. "I can't believe my good fortune," he hissed.

The monstrous creature laughed to himself as he began

plotting his revenge on the little-redheaded creature called 'Commander Leah.' He needed only to stun them both with his lightning and then he could recapture Qtrous as well. Gathering his energy, Stous began waving his arms to charge up his attack.

Suddenly, he felt another surge of electricity darting past him. He turned and saw Egosorous holding his stubby arms out in front of him, little bolts of lightning dancing between his scaly claws.

"I'll get her!" the creature growled, aiming at the two children.

"No!" growled Stous. "Stop!"

Too late. Egosorous smiled as the bolt of electricity left his claws and surged toward the two pink creatures in the distance.

Chapter 5

-Electrical Forces-

"What was that noise?" gasped Leah, spinning around on her heels. Her eyes nearly popped from her head as she saw the jagged line of electricity flying straight toward her. Frightened, she braced herself for the worst, but not much else. The bolt hit and Leah went down.

Leah shook her head and looked up, surprised to see Qtrous smiling down at her.

"Watch out," said the cloud creature. "The bolt was about to pierce—"

"Leah, watch out!" yelled Chris. Leah turned her head just in time to see him dive in front of another bolt of lightning.

The electric jolt wrapped around her brother, engulfing him in a glowing force of pure energy. He doubled over and shook wildly, then fell through the surface of the clouds below. Down he fell, through one layer of clouds after another, sinking like a boulder. Chris kicked his legs and waved his arms in the hope of grabbing something, as each layer of clouds he fell through shut behind him like a locked trap door. *Click, click, click.* Each layer echoed as he sunk deeper and deeper into trouble.

By the time Chris hit bottom with a thud, he'd lost count of how many layers he'd crossed. It felt as if he'd landed in a pile of snow. Jumping up, Christopher surveyed his surroundings. He could see hundreds of acres of frozen tundra with some of the weirdest cages imaginable. The hum coming from within the enclosures must be the moaning of the prisoners inside.

As he turned in a full circle, all he could see were cages. Crouching on one knee, he scratched the back of his head and felt his hair standing on end. He could feel the evil surrounding him as a perfect wedge of eight evil creatures pierced the grey clouds, flying low to drop their prisoners into the cages.

The snow started to rise from the floor. Christopher couldn't believe his eyes. Staring straight at him were some sort of snowflake soldiers. Each snowflake was wide, tall, and thin, resembling a playing card with two beady eyes.

Their legs, feet, and arms looked like stick men and their fingers like icicles. The most worrisome thing was that every snowflake emanated a strange, glowing energy in their icicle fingers, drawing their power from the cages.

Unlike the snowflakes back home, these all looked the same. In fact, they were all doing the same thing: marching straight toward him. Chris realized that the snowflakes were trying to encircle and trap him. He pulled his sword out to fend them off.

"Get back!" he yelled, and struck one of the snowflakes away with his sword.

It was an excellent strike, but the snowflake shocked his sword at the last moment, sending Chris to the ground feeling weak and dazed. There were too many of them. It was only a matter of time before they completely overran him. Stumbling to his feet, he shuffled toward the cages to make it harder for the snowflake soldiers to capture him. Looking inside the cages, he saw the ghostly shadows of the souls of children who had lost their dreams and lolled in a nightmare state.

"You fool!" screamed Stous, pointing an angry claw at

Egosorous. "I was about to spring my trap on all three of them. That Captain Christopher was nothing more than a delectable bonus for me!"

Egosorous stammered to come up with an answer.

"Now he has discovered my prison of souls!"

In the background, Rhinosorous snickered, enjoying seeing Stous yell at Egosorous.

Qtrous struggled to hold Leah as she fought to dive through the hole in the clouds left by her brother.

"Let me go!" she yelled, "I need to follow Captain Christopher. He might need my help.

"That's the not the best way," said Qtrous, swooping her up with his one, sail-like arm.

Together, they lifted into the air and soared over the clouds.

"We need to go. That was Stous or one of his minions who fired that bolt, and we don't want to stick around for his follow-up attack."

"But my brother—"

"Shh," said Qtrous as he steered through the sky. "Keep it down. They'll be looking for us and we won't be any good to Chris if they find us."

The force of her sobbing made her body rock back and forth uncontrollably. All she could see was the pain and fright in Christopher's delicate face. The fear in his eyes haunted her. *Oh, Christopher, come back. I'm so sorry for making you feel like a coward. I swear I'll never do it again. Please come back. You saved my life.*

"Qtrous, please take me to Artie."

Chapter 6

-New Addition-

Some distance away and above, Artie and Aero landed gently in Cloud City where they'd first taken Christopher and Leah days back. Before the magic carpet even stopped, Q and Lorous ran toward Artie as they jumped about and waved their arms.

"Where's Commander Leah?"

"Where's Captain Christopher!"

Artie groaned and held up his hand. "I'm sorry," he said solemnly, "but the last time I saw them, they were in the realm of Broken Clouds."

Lorous and Q stopped suddenly, looked at each other, and then screamed in unison, "WHAT?"

"Sorry, but it's true. There were some complications in the search for Qtrous. We found ourselves in the Orange Realm with Queen Ciella."

"Will she help us find them? And Qtrous?"

"Yes, she has pledged her help," smiled Artie. "As we speak, she's sending out emissaries to gather information and speed the search."

Lorous grabbed Artie. "I have terrible news. The Evil Eight came to the castle in Cloud Kingdom. They also got in and stole your chest. While protecting the castle, Mars and Clous were killed. " Tears fell as she related her new.

Arie stumbled and reached for his heart. "They will pay for this," Artie screamed in agony. They looked on as Artie tried to process the deaths of his friends. "The chest has not been opened yet. My magic is still holding out. Let us go."

The emissary bowed low.

"What news do you bring?" asked the angelic queen of the Orange Realm from her throne.

"Lord Mason of the Rainbow Causeway sends word," the emissary said. "He believes he has seen one of the creatures that you seek." The emissary removed a rolled scroll from his pouch and handed it to the queen with another bow.

"Excellent," said Queen Ciella, examining the scroll. "Send for Artie the elf. He is to meet me at the Wishbone Alley off the Rainbow Highway at once."

"As you command," said the emissary, stepping off to fulfill his queen's orders.

It took only minutes for the messengers to travel through the realms. In no time at all Artie and Aero appeared in a flurry of stardust at the queen's commanded meeting point. Wishbone Alley was empty and quiet when they arrived. Now with more precaution than ever, Artie set up a protection spell to keep them safe during the meeting.

With a sudden flash of bright orange and golden light, a sizeable halo-like rip appeared in the sky above Artie's head. An instant later, Queen Ciella drifted down through the opening and settled beside them in the nearby clouds.

Before a word could be exchanged, the Rainbow Causeway rumbled and shook, and the clouds beside Queen Ciella erupted with colored light. Slowly, majestically, the impressive figure of Lord Mason rose up with his regal wings that showed the many colors of the rainbow spread wide.

Lord Mason's massive muscular body was a mixture of a lion and the legendary Pegasus. His head had all the qualities of a lion but with human features. The ears were prominent and looked like miniature wings on the top of his head, partially hidden by his long, thick, white mane. His wings matched the color of his brilliant mane. These caressed his front forearms and were topped by golden clasps. Strapped to his back was a white shield. On his tail, legs, and front forearms he wore golden multi bands and bracelets.

"Queen Ciella," said Lord Mason with a slight bow, "And Artie the elf. It's good to see both of you again. You and your adventures are spoken of throughout the Causeway."

"It's a wonder," smiled Queen Ciella. "We have been busier since our adventurers Christopher and Leah arrived."

"So, what can I do for the both of you?" asked Lord Mason.

Artie checked the stability of his protective spell and then stepped forward to speak.

"Aggh!" yelled Egosorous, situated a good distance from Artie and his companions. "That stupid elf is starting to get wise to us listening in on him!" With one angry swipe, he knocked away the magic clouds that usually allowed him to spy on people from far away. "He must be using some protective spell," he mumbled, turning to Rhinosorous. "You!" he pointed at the beastly creature. "Get down there and find out what they're up to!"

Egosorous finished the order with a kick, sending Rhinosorous to his feet. The big creature bowed reluctantly and exited.

Safe within the protective bubble, Artie addressed Lord Mason. "Some of my friends have gotten tangled up with Stous," he said grimly.

"Stous!" growled Lord Mason. "Don't they know that you can't mess with him and live to tell about it?"

"Believe it or not, they've escaped him at least once," said Artie.

"Then they were lucky to do so."

Artie grinned briefly. "I know. And they were torn away from us when they entered the realm of Broken Clouds."

Lord Mason shook his head in disbelief. "Either they're very courageous and smart," said Lord Mason, "or very dumb. No one returns from there. And I mean *no one*."

Lord Mason's eyes widened as he looked at Queen Ciella. "Wait. Do you mean to tell me that the girl I saw in my blue bow was one of them?"

"Indeed," Queen Ciella nodded.

Artie swept forward and pleaded with Lord Mason for help. "Please! Can you tell us exactly where you saw her? Anything you can tell us about her whereabouts will help!"

Lord Mason nodded. "Of course."

Chapter 7

-News-

"I know the one you call Commander Leah and she is just fine. Much to my surprise, I saw her floating past on the blue bow after you say she disappeared into the realm of Broken Clouds. As Lord of the Rainbow Causeway, I am the only one who can see in the blue bow."

Artie nodded.

"I did not see Captain Christopher, however," Lord Mason added. "Although you should know that the blue bow stopped its journey somewhere in a realm beyond our own."

A smile stretched across Artie's face. "Yes!" he stammered. "It must be Planet Earth, the realm of Children! The blue bow must have taken them home!"

"I believe their mission through the Broken Clouds was a success," Queen Ciella said. "Against all odds, I might add."

Lord Mason looked ready to agree, then suddenly stopped and stared grimly into the distance. "Their escape from the Broken Clouds did succeed," he said, "but I've just received some disturbing news."

"Pray tell," said Artie. "Speak the words, Lord Mason."

Lord Mason lowered his head and closed his eyes for a moment. "I have been notified by my scouting parties that Commander Leah and Qtrous are in Stratocloudous."

"That's unwelcome news," Artie mumbled.

"What of Captain Christopher?" asked Queen Ciella.

Lord Mason hesitated. "That is a different matter, I'm sorry to say."

"What is it?" asked Queen Ciella and Artie in unison.

"Captain Christopher has been hit by an energy force by one of Stous's minions, Egosorous. Christopher is alive and trapped in a land where the sun won't shine."

Artie swallowed hard before whispering, "Not

Tundrasorous?"

Lord Mason nodded.

"A terrible shame," Queen Ciella said. "Once such a beautiful land. A paradise."

"Before Stous laid it to waste," added Artie. "Now nothing grows there. Not even the sun will touch it. Only two strange moons light this realm."

"And the creatures that dwell in Tundrasorous," Lord Mason said, "are frightful indeed. They surround anyone who finds himself there and stun him with their electrified fingers."

"We can't think he is lost to us," Artie said sternly. "That's not acceptable! We must help him!"

Queen Ciella reached out and grabbed Artie by the shoulder. "Calm yourself, Artie. We need to be careful, calm, and collected to figure out how to deal with this."

They all stood for a moment in thought.

"We are getting ready to send out a search party for the elders. They will go down to Tundrasorous. This plan can be two-fold: to find the children and rescue Captain Christopher," Queen Ciella said.

"March!" came the straightforward order to attack the intruder.

Finding cover against the onslaught of marching soldiers, Christopher slowly crept backward to position himself behind one of the cages. All the while, he kept eye contact with the soldiers.

In this two-moon realm, the snow was as hard as diamonds in some areas and like a cool slushy drink in others. It was like quicksand once you were in it, and by then, it was too late.

Christopher felt himself slip. Adrenaline pumped straight to his heart with a thud. His head pounded and sweat rolled off his forehead as his armpits chilled from the mixture of sweat and cold tundra air. He caught himself with his other foot just before losing his balance and silently thanked God. Suddenly, the snow ledge snapped off. Christopher's stomach did a flip-flop as the floor fell out from under him. His arms flew straight in the air as he lost his balance and his sword. He saw the last glimmer of light shine on the blade as it fell into the vast depths of the pit.

He spiraled downward and landed on his side, one shoulder seeming to touch the other like an accordion. The sudden crash sucked his stomach into his back while his lungs depressed and let out all the air. It felt as though the blood drained from his brain. All went black.

Christopher lay there lifeless until a heavenly light shone upon the blade of his sword with such brightness that it pierced his eyes. Christopher blinked and shook his head, trying to wake up. The light continued to pierce his eyes. "My sword..." Quivering inside, Christopher tried to sit up.

He rested against the cold wall made of ice and snow and checked to see if he could move any further. He hurt from head to toe but nothing seemed broken. He slid one knee under him and pushed himself up the side of the ice wall. Pain engulfed his body and rumbled through his brain like a freight train. A small trickle of blood slipped past his lips. His breath came in painful gasps. As he wiped the blood from his mouth, he grinned. There was his sword not twenty-five feet away. He covered the distance and had just grabbed a sword when a soldier zapped him with a jolt of electricity. It shot through him like a bolt of lightning, causing his body to shake and spasm. As the soldier approached for the final shock, Christopher bolted forward and knocked his attacker over the ledge.

Regaining his composure, Christopher smiled. *Good riddance.* He picked up his sword again and looked around. His breath came in hot short bursts and each gasp brought more pain thanks to the bruises that covered him. The cold ice wall cut and scratched his hands as he felt his way across it. With his sword, he cut footholds into the ice and began his climb up the ice wall. Every muscle rebelled against him, yet he continued to move closer to the top.

The wall shook with a force that rumbled through his hands and feet.

"Now what?" he cried. The air seemed to ripple around him as the wall collapsed. Falling downward into a mixture of ice and snow, he rolled to a halt. Christopher looked about as his eyes adjusted to the darkness. He thought he saw twinkles of light in different places. "Good grief, now I'm seeing things." As he shuffled toward an opening in the cavern, he could feel the cold seeping into his shoes and up his legs.

He put his head down, feeling alone. Where were Leah, Artie, and the others? He had come to rely on them so much, and now he felt utterly alone, full of fear, and lost. No one knew where he was. Help was not coming. He slumped onto the floor in despair.

Heavy sobs overcame him. Thoughts and pictures flashed through his mind of the times the bullies took his stuff, made fun of him because he was so smart, thought he was weak when he was just being kind and understanding, or laughed at him because he couldn't play baseball well.

He shook his head as he yelled, "No, no, no. Not today. I'm in no mood for this." Christopher felt something go through him and thought about the times he'd helped the weaker kids and how he went to battle against the Evil Eight and their overlord. He remembered how he saved Leah. Finally, he stood up again and continued to bumble through the tunnel until he heard a trickling noise. He readjusted his path and followed the sound into an opening to a small body of water. "How could there be water moving inside this tundra realm?" Christopher drew closer. An intense heat rose off the water. At the bottom was a core as red as the sun. Here was the beginning of the creation of this realm.

The closer he got, the stronger he felt. He noticed his sword start to hum and glow, as did the water covering the core. His mind, body, and spirit were ignited with a power that coursed through him. He needed a way out. His eyes lit upon a small, thin opening in the walls through which the snowflake soldiers traveled in and out. Christopher used his sword to expand the chamber wall.

Artie had said that the same power that created the realms forged this sword. Inside he saw the tiny steps of a staircase spiraling upward. Rejuvenated by hope and believing in himself and the power that created the sword, he began the long, hard climb up the stairwell.

Chapter 8

– *The Librarian* –

"First," Queen Ciella continued, "we should use the blue bow of the rainbow to rescue Leah and Qtrous. We will be invisible to our enemies until it's too late for them to reach us. Rescuing them first should eliminate the easier problem and give us more people to work on rescuing Christopher."

Lord Mason shook his head. "Once you're in the Blue Realm, you'll become invisible. However, you won't be able to break through the time-space field that protects the blue archway that allows you into Stratocloudous."

"Well, there must be some way," exclaimed Artie.

"I believe there is." Lord Mason said. "I will examine the old ways, written before the foundations came about. Perhaps they hold a secret." Lord Mason opened his wings. "It will take some time. I will return once I've finished."

With a flourish of his wings and a touch of rainbow dust, Lord Mason vanished.

Far from the meeting place, Lord Mason appeared in the entryway of an ancient library. The walls were made of worn clouds, hard like a brick, and lined with countless shelves of books and scrolls. It was the holder of all archives and maps, books, and knowledge before the times of the realms and ruled by Liam, the librarian.

Liam was an odd Cloud creature, his shape that of two funnel clouds end to end, with a large opening to accommodate his large head that was capable of storing enormous amounts of information. Another large opening pointed towards the ground to accommodate his legs and feet. Where the two points connected, his arms sprouted outwards.

All the wisdom of the realms came and went through his magnificent brain. His eyes were large and bright offset by a gentle smile. Topping his head was a spiked hairdo that looked like a crown.

"Lord Mason?" a voice echoed through the halls. "I haven't seen you in…what? Four centuries? I thought we were friends."

Lord Mason turned to see the cloud librarian, Liam, floating toward him. "Of course, we're friends," Lord

Mason smiled, "and it has been far too long."

The two bowed to each other as old friends, laughing and smiling as they did.

"I could use your help, Liam. I have a delicate task of the greatest importance."

"And what would that be?" Liam asked.

"I need to find a back way into Tundrasorous."

Liam jumped back. "Oh my! Why would anyone want to go there?"

Lord Mason frowned. "A worthwhile question, indeed. I have friends who need to rescue someone from there. A child creature, no less. Also, we believe that it has become a prison for the souls of missing creatures throughout the realms. The elders have sent emissaries to the Council for help, but more children have been going missing at an alarming rate since Stous formed the Evil Eight."

"Well, then!" smiled Liam, "At least when you decide to come back, you bring me something interesting!"

"Interesting? But not impossible?"

"No, no. Surely not," said Liam, floating over to a pile

of old, rolled papers. The cloud creature removed several scrolls from the pile and pointed them toward Lord Mason.

"Here," he said, "these maps should help. They are old maps, ancient maps of the realms and all of the old passageways between."

Lord Mason took the maps and began unrolling them on a nearby table.

"Now remember," Liam continued, "Tundrasorous is full of nasty little snowflake soldiers. They were the only survivors after Stous ruined everything with his terrible deeds and corruption."

"I remember. It all happened after Stous was cast down to Stratocloudous as punishment for trying to take control of all the realms. That was never meant to be, but his greed and lust for power have always been insatiable."

"A truly terrible story," Liam nodded. "Once, Tundrasorous was a wondrous place full of beauty, second only to heaven itself. Then Stous put an end to that by turning it into a frozen, dark place. But if nothing else, we know that Stous himself found a backdoor into Tundrasorous for his prison of souls. That, my friend, is the good news you need to hear."

"Yes," nodded Lord Mason, looking at the maps carefully. "That back door is what we need now."

Liam nodded and then chuckled. "And let us pray that Stous never finds a way out of Stratocloudous and into these peaceful realms."

Lord Mason looked up from the maps and frowned. "It hasn't happened in thousands of years. I hope it will never come to that."

Chapter 9

–Hooray for Backdoors–

Lord Mason looked back at the map, and his eyes widened. "This!" he exclaimed, pointing to the paper. "Here is the back door. I will need to fly through the space-time archway."

Liam squinted. "Hmm. Only a few creatures have that power, and you will need to find it. I have an elf friend with a flying carpet who may know—"

Lord Mason grinned. "Artie?"

"Yes! Artie! Do you know him as well, Lord Mason?"

"Indeed. I will see Artie immediately. Artie will be happy to see these maps you have provided. Thank you, old friend!"

"It was my pleasure. Good luck on your journey!"

The two old friends bowed once more, and Lord Mason disappeared with a flurry of his wings and rainbow-colored clasps.

Artie and Queen Ciella became silent as Lord Mason materialized nearby.

"I have good news, but dangerous news," he said. "There is a back door to Tundrasorous, but it takes us between the two most dangerous realms known to our kind, Tundrasorous and Stratocloudous."

Artie and Queen Ciella both looked frightened at the prospect. Everyone knew of Tundrasorous and how it had come into being.

"What must be done must be done," Artie said, stiffening his jaw.

"Then gather round and let me explain what's needed to complete this quest."

Lord Mason quickly explained the path from one realm to the next, using Liam's map to show the course.

At the end of the explanation, Lord Mason asked Artie, "Do you know any magical creature that can travel through the time-space barrier?"

Artie smiled. "I do. I have just the friends."

The elf summoned Aero and instructed the magic carpet to find Elephantous.

"Once we have Qtrous and Leah," Artie explained, "there will be too many for you to carry alone, Aero."

Aero nodded his tassels in agreement, bowed, and flew into the distance.

"Now," added Lord Mason, "let's finish this plan without delay. We should leave as soon as he returns."

Aero returned moments later with Elephantous following behind.

Chapter 10

-Cosmic Gut Check-

At the very edge of Cloud Kingdom, the scouting party and the companions stood peering over the endless vastness of the realms. Artie, Queen Ciella, Lord Mason, Oda, Paola, Aero, and Elephantous, each felt a measure of fear and insignificance in comparison to the vastness.

Without a word, Artie put his hand in front of him. Followed by Paola, Oda, Lord Mason, and Queen Ciella above his. Aero placed his shimmering magic tassel on top of their hands, and finally, Elephantous's trunk topped the stack.

"We do this because duty calls," said Artie, "and we are doers!"

Raising their hands above their heads, everyone shouted in unison: "Until the end!"

With that, Elephantous trumpeted and the sound echoed throughout the realms.

Artie smiled. "We are ready!"

Lord Mason raised his hand and directed the blue bow of a rainbow toward the narrow cavern between Stratocloudous and Tundrasorous. On his signal, everyone jumped onto the blue band and traveled quick as lightning to a destination that had been hundreds of miles in the distance only a second earlier. The party arrived safely at the location of the back door, between the two most dangerous realms in the kingdom.

"Liam?" asked Lord Mason, squinting at a figure floating nearby.

"Yes, Lord Mason!" said the cloud creature, smiling. "I decided to make sure the map location was correct. I've examined this spot, and it seems like the back door is intact."

"That's excellent news."

"Besides," Liam added, floating his way next to the group, "I couldn't let you have all the fun."

Lord Mason chuckled. "Very good,"

"Although I must add something. A bit of bad news that I discovered while examining the area."

Artie massaged the back of his neck awaiting the news. Queen Ciella stood up and demanded, "Well...out with it!"

He turned his head to the side, avoiding her eyes. "One of your child creatures is most certainly in Tundrasorous. Christopher. He's trapped and it doesn't look good for him."

The party gasped in unison and questions began flying from every mouth. The most important question came loudly over the rest: "Is he still alive?"

Shadows covered the Council and they felt evil approaching. Looking upward, they saw the Evil Eight swoooping down upon the Council with weapons drawn. Attack after attack came so swiftly that the Council could barely hold them off.

As the attackers regrouped, Morgan screeched, "These are no ordinary creatures!"

"I know," Spike replied, "they are blocking my daggers. No one has ever been able to do that."

"They have neutralized our special powers," Lovonous said.

Artie, the Elf, stood defensively, awaiting the next wave of attacks. "Where did these creatures come from?" he gasped. "I have never seen such fighting abilities and weapons."

"Stay alert," Queen Ciella said. "These appear to be the Evil Eight."

"There will be another attack and very soon," Lord Mason said.

Lucian applied his invisibility and flew toward the Council to see if he could spy on them. He overheard their gasps of shock and returned to the others.

"They are just as surprised as we are. I believe they are expecting another attack," Lucian said.

"Let's give it to them," Venous said with a grin.

"No, retreat, we need a plan," Morgan said.

"Where are they?" the queen shouted.

"Leave them. We need to get out of here and save Christopher," Artie shouted.

"We don't even know if he is alive," Lord Mason yelled.

"He was when I saw him," was all that Liam could say.

"Then we need to move quickly. The plan must change. We must rescue Christopher first," Lord Mason said.

"No," Artie interrupted, "I don't think we can spare any time rescuing Leah and Qtrous, either. Both are in danger, so we must split up."

"It's a good thing so many have joined our rescue," said Queen Ciella.

Artie nodded and began to divide the group.

"Wait a minute," Oda asked. "What about us and our mission?"

"Well, I can tell you that if the Evil Eight is here and guarding this backdoor, your children will share the same fate as Captain Christopher if we don't get in there to help," Artie said.

"I'll take Aero, Elephantous, Oda, and Paola with me. Queen Ciella and Lord Mason, you should go with Liam."

"Very well," said Liam, "but let me show you this map of Stratocloudous where Lord Mason last saw Leah and Qtrous." Liam pointed out the precise location and added a warning: "The surface of the clouds has changed a lot, and the maps need to be updated, so be careful. Roads and passages may have shifted a good deal. The good news is that your friends are in an area with much wind and dust so they may have no trouble staying hidden."

"It will also make them harder for us to find," said Artie.

Liam nodded. "Perhaps…but now for our mission. We must make haste. If these maps are correct, the creatures in Tundrasorous have nearly gotten Christopher to their prison. Once inside all chances of rescue will be lost."

Chapter 11

-2 x Teamwork-

"Well mates," said Liam, "we should synchronize our realm time. The only way to do this is to stand in a special place that will draw time from all realms."

Liam unrolled several smaller maps and quickly skimmed them. A moment later, he was pointing out special places for each party member to stand. Pulling out his chronometer, he pushed down on its stem. "There," he said once everyone was in place, "we are synchronized."

"Okay, let's hurry. Artie, count to fifteen before your group flies into Stratocloudous. We're not flying, so we need the lead." With that, Lord Mason directed the blue bow to Tundrasorous, and he, Queen Ciella, and Liam departed on the beam of light.

Artie performed the countdown, "…thirteen, fourteen, fifteen…go!" He steered Aero through the time-space archway that Liam had examined.

Elephantous followed directly behind. Together, they appeared in the realm of Stratocloudous, landing in the middle of such a terrible storm that various creatures clung to spinning clouds for dear life.

Taking cover, Artie shouted over the tornado wall of spinning clouds to Elephantous, "Point us toward where you dropped them off!"

Elephantous indicated the direction, and they all departed that way.

"Keep your eyes open for traps or ambushes," Artie said, his head low to avoid the harsh wind. No sooner had Artie said that than a flying wedge of pure wickedness descended upon the Council.

The Evil Eight screeched out a victory call. "Where is your magic, Artie, the Elf? Your chest is ours, and we will have it opened soon. We have been waiting for you." Cackling sounds echoed off the winds.

Artie yelled, "Circle up now."

Oda, Paolo, Artie, and Elephantous circled in a counterclockwise direction while Aero flew high above. As the circle of the Council concentrated on the Evil Eight flying above, they missed the two minions attacking from their left.

The first arrow flew wide of Paola but hit Elephantous, with a *fth-ump*. Elephantous raised high on his massive gorilla legs and let out a mighty trumpeted scream. The arrow was a mere inconvenience. He grabbed it and broke it off. He spun and broke ranks yelling, "Paola, are you okay?"

She nodded quickly.

Elephantous yelled, "Hey, Artie I'll take the one with the bow and arrow."

"Make sure he doesn't get back up," Artie replied.

"That won't be a problem."

"You get all the fun," Oda yelled above the cackling.

Elephantous grabbed hold of the minion, lifted him high into the air, and slammed him down over his knee. He spun around and threw him at the Evil Eight that were circling above. If it hadn't been for the quick thinking of Morgan, Elephantous would have had a strike. Artie quickly closed the circle in time to fend off the first wave of attack.

The singed air crackled while Morgan's fire lead the group downward, hiding their next attack. Out of the flames came daggers in all direction from Spike. Artie moved around the circle and cast his magic spell causing the attack to fail.

Artie motioned. "Stay close."

Spike's daggers were deflected. Some hit the ground with a thud while others clinked and clanged against each other, deflecting wide of their target.

Spike watched his daggers fail and yelled to Ripkin, "Do something."

Ripkin raised his arms in front of him, palms outward, and waved his right arm clockwise, his left arm counterclockwise. The wind whirled into a funnel, and Ripkin let it loose on the Evil Eight, engulfing them in a force field, as they dropped into the circle.

The Council spun around and attacked. Venous went for her sword to attack, but a bow cracked her hand before she could draw it from its sheath.

Paola smiled. "Not so fast," she said, waving her finger. Paola suddenly went down from a crack to her head.

Oda bent to pick her up but turned to block the next dagger that flew past his nose. Artie countered with a magic fireball that blew Droll, Lucian, and Zererous out of the circle and left them unconscious. Aero flew in and picked up Paola.

Elephantous grabbed two of the Evil Eight. It looked to be Morgan and Venous and with his massive arms, smashed them both together. "Let's see how hard your heads are."

With a thud, they went down.

"Hmm, not that hard after all."

Oda grabbed Ripken by his wing and nearly ripped it off as he took to the air and wobbled out of sight.

Artie caught the dagger two inches in front of his face. He turned and smiled at Spike. "I see you have not been inside my chest. With all your talk, your overlord isn't strong enough. Now begone and tell him I'm coming for what is mine."

As the last minion stood before them, an arrow pierced his upper leg, and he fell to his knees. The Council looked about in surprise as Leah and Qtrous appeared from around the cloud wall.

Qtrous reached down and took the dagger from behind his back. "He was getting ready to throw this," Qtrous shouted above the storm.

"I knew you would come for us. I just knew it!" Leah said.

Everyone came together in one giant hug, all smiles, and laughter, while Aero and Paola flew happy circles above their heads.

"Artie," said Leah with sudden realization, "I know you just got here, but something happened to Christopher, and we need to act fast…"

"Did I just hear one of those child creatures?" Rhinosorous whispered to himself, slowing down as he strolled along through the cloud floor. He quickly changed direction, floating back to where he thought he heard the voice of a girl. Once he neared the spot, he sank lower into the cloud floor where he could travel undetected. It was something Egosorous didn't know he could do.

"Don't worry," said a voice that sounded like an elf, "we have friends looking for Captain Christopher. We will be joining them as soon as we get you out of here."

"Then let's go!" came the girl's voice.

Just as Rinosorous thought, it was the creature and the elf.

"Get on Aero with Qtrous and Oda and me," said Artie. "Paola can ride out on Elephantous. Now let's fly!"

Rhinosorous waited a moment before poking his head out to see. The creatures were all flying away, including the child creature that Stous was so intent on finding. Rhinosorous snickered to himself, "If I let them get away, Egosorous will get blamed. Stous will probably destroy him for that and then I will be next in command!"

Flying low along the clouds to avoid the wind, Artie leaned over to Leah and shouted, "There's one more thing we need to do while we're down here."

"What's that?" she yelled back over the howl.

"Get back something you had stolen from you!"

Artie grinned and brought his hands together with a thunderous clap. A swirling, shining ball of magical energy formed around his hands, and with a flourish, Artie let the orb of energy fly. The ball exploded forward, arcing into the distance and landing somewhere out of sight with a wicked screech and rolling blast.

Leah heard the howl of a cloud creature being struck by the energy—she thought it sounded like Stous.

A second later, the ball of glowing energy returned to Artie's waiting hands. He caught something and opened his palms to show Leah. Her breath caught. Between his fingers were the two missing amulets, along with one of Stous's slimy, long claws.

"There," smirked Artie, "now we can go."

"Master, you let them take the amulet," Egosorous said in surprise.

With anger and disgust in his eyes, Stous said, "Yes, I did, and I had to sacrifice one of my claws to do so."

"But why?"

"I needed them to have the amulet."

"I don't understand. Why not just give it to them in another way?"

"It had to be believable; it's all part of my plan."

Chapter 12

–*Double Cross*–

Stous screamed in agony, clutching his injured hand, and paced back and forth in front of a smoking hole in the cavern wall.

"Where are you, Egosorous!" he shouted.

Rhinosorous slithered up to Stous and said with a grin, "I think I just saw him over there." He then pointed to the spot where he'd encountered the girl and her friends.

A moment later, Egosorous reentered the cavern. "Yes, Stous?" he said with a bow.

"Did you find those creatures?"

"No, of course not. I've been in the next cavern working with the Evil Eight about how to deal with the Council."

Rhinosorous jumped up and pointed an accusing

finger, avoiding Stous's glance and smiling at Egosorous. "Not true! I saw you scouting the area over there…right where that ball of energy came from!"

Stous frowned, revealing rows of sharp teeth as he gave a deafening roar.

Meanwhile, Lord Mason, Queen Ciella, and Liam gazed at the unique mirrored map that showed their reflection as well as the territory of Tundrasorous and began their exploration of Tundrasorous. Shortly after arriving, they'd spotted a strong electrical current in the distance.

"I cannot use my rainbows within this realm," Lord Mason scowled. "We need another way."

"I've found a cloud that will take us to the prison," said Liam. "But we need to get to it, first."

"I can get us to the cloud," said Queen Ciella, "but my powers will only work once when we are in this realm. Are we sure this is the best use of them?"

Liam shrugged. "If we don't get to the prison, the rescue is over anyway. We must do what we must to get there."

Queen Ciella nodded. "Prepare yourselves," she said, waving her hands above her head.

In seconds, the winds began to rise and howl. Clouds moved and swirled, now with a cloud force field surrounding them. They started to drill down through the electrified clouds of Tundrasorous and toward their destination. When they emerged from the other side, the party found themselves staring at a horde of snowflake soldiers heading toward them.

"Blast!" shouted Queen Ciella. "They managed to put me off course!"

"How far off course?" Lord Mason demanded.

"I can't tell," Liam answered.

"Can you plot us a course to get back on track? Those soldiers will be upon us in seconds if we don't—" Lord Mason twisted in time to avoid the electric shock from the soldier as he struck. He disposed of the soldier quickly.

Liam looked through his maps then quickly pointed toward the horizon. "That way! About 320 rods to travel."

Lord Mason turned and scowled. "Speak so we can all understand, Liam!"

"About a mile."

"Then we move! Quickly!" said Queen Ciella, leading the way.

The three made it through the first cavern with haste. After crossing over the second rise, it seemed that the group had avoided the soldiers. The final leg of their trip took them through a long, winding cave.

"The prison will be just beyond this exit!" said Liam as they neared the end.

Suddenly, a blast of electricity shook the cave, sending cloud balls flying in every direction. With a shudder and crackle of energy, the cave exit collapsed.

"Now what?" Liam asked.

"I knew I should have saved my powers."

Lord Mason frowned at Queen Ciella. "Yes, instead of wasting them getting us lost in the first place."

Queen Ciella's face reddened, and she looked ready to scream at Lord Mason, but she calmed herself and raised her hand peacefully. "Wait a moment," she said. "We're already bickering and picking fights amongst ourselves. That is the twisted power of this place; the confusion and distortion Stous left behind."

"You're right," said Lord Mason. "I'm sorry for my remark," he added with a humble bow.

"Well, since we don't have many options, I think I should try this gadget I've been working on," said Liam. "It will either save the day or make things much worse."

Before anyone could react, Liam removed a small device from his pocket and placed it near the collapsed exit. He dashed backward and pressed a button on a remote control in his other hand.

Lord Mason and Queen Ciella covered their eyes, fearing the worst, but the device merely hummed and emitted a glow of light and energy. A split-second later, the device produced a glowing rod of light that expanded into a five-star pattern. Through the pattern, Lord Mason could see the prison.

"A makeshift archway!" he gasped. "Well done, Liam!"

Liam smiled and ran through the star-shaped portal. Queen Ciella and Lord Mason followed. On the other side, they emerged beyond the cave to the sound of electricity. With that, a burst of light and thunder ripped a hole in the sky above them. Through shielded eyes, the party could see Commander Leah, Aero, and Artie, Oda, Paolo, Qtrous, and Elephantous, each flying through the passage. They quickly descended to ground level to meet up with the others.

"You've made it just in time," yelled Lord Mason. "We can hear the screeching and pained moans of a wounded animal or worse, of Christopher."

They lowered their heads and avoided eye contact with one another.

Chapter 13

Tundrasorous

Leah's eyes widened and she acted immediately. "Aero," she said, spurring the carpet into motion, "to Christopher's side...NOW!"

Aero departed so quickly that Artie rolled off, landing nimbly on his feet at Lord Mason's side, his eyes wide with surprise. "What passion these humans have," he said shaking his head in awe.

It took only an instant for the magic carpet to carry Leah to the prison wall, and even less time for them both to land on the other side with a loud thud.

Leah shook off the landing and looked around. Nearby was her brother, Captain Christopher, but between them stood an army of snowflake soldiers. The soldiers crackled with electricity, and they were determined to finish off the captain.

"Stop!" yelled Leah.

Every snowflake soldier stopped and turned to look

at her.

"Uh-oh," she whispered. She heaved a sigh of relief when the rest of her companions slowly descended to her side, carried over the wall by a strained but willing Elephantous.

"You are too late!" came a voice in Leah's head, unspoken by anyone, but as loud as a shout.

The Council members heard it and looked at each other.

She watched as the snowflake general moved toward Christopher, ready to deliver the most potent and lethal shock possible.

"No!" Leah called out, but her word was cut short by an explosion of light and heat so powerful that it seemed like the sun itself had appeared.

Leah shielded her eyes and then blinked through the flash to see every snowflake soldier melting to nothing where they stood. Every cage had gone dark. Leah dove forward, covering her brother and protecting his eyes with her arm. The heat and light ended a second later, fading away as if it had never been.

"What happened?" Artie yelled, picking himself up from the ground.

Leah was too busy lifting Christopher to his feet to answer.

"Oh man," he moaned, rubbing at his eyelids. He tried to catch his breath as tears formed at the corners of his eyes, his lips trembled, and his heart pounded.

"That was close, but I kept the faith. I knew somehow you'd find me."

Christopher smiled and wobbled to his feet.

Leah grabbed his arm and held him upright. "Oh, Chris, I am so sorry I ever doubted you." She hugged Christopher and spun him around.

Artie heard Lord Mason say, "That light…was me," brushing himself off. "I took a chance and used a power I've never tried before. I had to gamble that it wouldn't kill us all."

Everyone's eyes went wide, and they yelled in unison, "What did you do?"

"I connected all of the colors of the rainbow. Compressed them into one streak of light. Blue has never touched orange. Violet has never touched red, and so on. I think I may have short-circuited the entire atmosphere of the realm."

"But everyone is alright it seems," said Queen Ciella.

Everyone nodded in turn.

"Wow," said Christopher as he squinted and pointed upward. "Look!"

The Council felt a sudden burst of heat as a newly formed sun appeared in the sky. All around them they felt the ground shift as clouds of green grass formed and trees began to spout.

A figure dressed in white appeared from out of the trees. With a youthful countenance and a bow, he said, "Welcome to Utopia. My name is Prince Nolan."

The Council surrounded Prince Nolan with greetings and questions.

"All questions will be answered in time. I know that you have pressing matters to attend to. We'll see each other soon." With that and a bow, he was gone.

"Okay," Artie cut in, "we need to get out of here."

"Aye," said Lord Mason. "Let's mount up and fly."

Through clouds and dust, away from the prison, they flew together. As they exited Tundrasorous, the entire party shared the same space as Stratocloudous for a brief instant. At that moment, the attack came.

The Evil Eight swooped in a perfect stealth wedge and attacked. Taken by surprise, the Council sustained minor injuries on the first go around. Gathering themselves, they went into their formation.

"Prepare yourselves! Here they come again," Artie yelled.

There was a natural pairing of super strength. Captain Christopher found himself locked in battle with one of the most dangerous opponents he'd ever faced, Venous. Nothing could compare to her sword fighting abilities. With a deft paring stroke, she cut into Christopher's arm. Swinging on the backstroke, she almost ended Christopher. He moved quickly and only lost his new hat, not his head.

"Nice move, brother," said Leah as she grabbed her bow.

"Thanks," Christopher added as he grabbed for his hat that was no longer there.

Lord Mason sprang into action with wings widespread and captured fire and ice, causing Morgan and Droll to collapse into each other as they went down. Pouncing, Lord Mason made short work of them.

Spike's dagger flew true at Artie, but the elf's internal radar went off and opened his force field at the last moment. The point of the blade got through, but no more. Ripken charged with his force field and collapsed Artie's protection, leaving Artie vulnerable to Spike's next attack.

Leah drew back an arrow, the shaft shimmering against the bow. Releasing the arrow, it flew true, hitting its target. Spike went down before he could hurl his dagger.

"Close call, Artie," Leah yelled.

"So it was, thank you. Now watch yourself," Artie replied.

Ripken quickly withdrew his force field from Artie and shielded himself against the onslaught of Leah's arrows. Lovonous grabbed Oda from behind to take him down and crush him, but Oda was too powerful and repelled the attack. Lovonous lost the element of surprise and Oda swung around, grabbed Lovonous by the neck and started to squeeze.

"Are you surprised to find someone else with the same strength as you?" Oda said.

"You're not as strong as I am!" Lovonous cried. Breaking the hold, Lovonous moved in closer with the intention of reaching into his chest cavity and pulling out his heart. "You're just a little wimp."

Oda also moved in close, whispering the words, "this wimp is now going to end you."

Lovonous's eyes went wide with the sudden pain as he froze like a pillar of salt.

Christopher parried Venous's next strike with one of his own, then jumped up and over his enemy. Christopher brought down his sword in one deft move and Venous's head rolled gently to the ground. "You'll not be needing my hat anymore," he said as he placed it back on top of his head.

Lucian and Zererous teamed up to take on Paola

when Queen Ciella waved her hands, and Lucian became visible right in front of Paola. With lightning speed, Paola sidestepped the attack from Lucian, while Liam blasted him with a red-hot laser beam.

Paola looked over at Queen Ciella. "That's what I call teamwork."

Liam nodded as Queen Ciella said, "We all have to stick together."

Zererous snickered as he investigated Queen Ciella and saw her weakness. Her powers were not strong down here and they had to charge before using them again. Taking advantage, Zererous brought down his sword, clipping her mane as she moved away quick as a cat. The loud screech followed—the result of Leah's arrow piercing Zerorous. The Council took to the realms, leaving their enemy in defeat. Just as they cleared Stratocloudous, they could see a giant, slimy claw reaching through space. It was missing one bony finger.

"Stous!" Leah shrieked.

The claw snatched at them, then whipped sideways to slice deep into Artie's flesh. As fast as it appeared, it was gone again. Leah and Aero hurried the injured elf to the safe realm of Cloud Kingdom. Artie stumbled off Aero and fell to his knees. Queen Ciella reached out to hold him steady.

"Oh no," Christopher said.

Queen Ciella laid Artie on the ground. "Take off his armor," she commanded.

The wound was wide open. Artie was losing precious elven blood.

Lord Mason looked on with anxiety. Seeing Artie's face answered his concerns. Leah watched Lord Mason's reaction, and tears welled in her eyes.

Cradling Artie's head, Christopher yelled, "Hold on! You must hold on."

Queen Ciella bent next to Christopher and looked deep into Artie's eyes. Her hands moved as quick as a surgeon, applying pressure here and checking there. Compassion changed to action. "I must get my elixir," Queen Ciella said.

Every member of the Council looked on. The silence spoke as clearly as the sight of Artie lying there. Queen Ciella looked up and scanned each set of eyes watching her with pure desperation.

The overshadowing light told the story. The atmosphere was changing and darkness was moving in fast. Goosebumps appeared on their arms yet there was no breeze. Or was there? Everything seemed surreal.

"The elixir," Queen Ciella said. She clapped her hands and disappeared. A moment later at the Rainbow Causeway, she scanned for the orange bow. Her foot found it and she bolted forward. Her golden mane flew over her head and whipped back across her face as she flew through the air with great force. Prous had hit her dead center. Queen Ciella slammed to a full stop.

"You're not going anywhere," Ripkin hissed. His hot breath heated her neck.

Queen Ciella felt as if she were in a vice.

The soldier squeezed harder and whispered, "You're not going to help that elf or anyone else."

Trembling, Lord Mason knelt by Christopher's side and whispered, "Don't worry, Christopher. The queen will be back." Running his hand through Artie's hair, Lord Mason looked desperate. Tears flooded his hollow blackened eyes. "Please, let's give Artie room."

"Without a miracle, he will pass," said one of the Council members."

Christopher turned and yelled, "That can't be. I won't let it." He took off his coat and placed it under Artie's head.

Leah shook her head as more tears fell. Paola looked on in fear.

Oda asked Liam, "Can elixir help at this stage?"

Darkness surrounded them. All voices and sound went mute. The silence was suffocating. Lord Mason let out a royal roar as Elephantous trumpeted a loud sad note. *Where is Queen Ciella?*

Some distance away, Queen Ciella managed to grab Ripken's wrist and force it back while she twisted it. Ripken screamed in pain and released her. She escaped only to find herself whipping around inside a giant net.

"Prous!"

She struggled to get free, but the web tightened,

sending blood pumping through her head. The blackout was close. Precious moments rushed through the time portal. Queen Ciella had to hurry to get the elixir. She tried her magic powers again but to no avail. With her head pounding and her body under crushing pressure, Queen Ciella heard Prous's voice.

"Stous wants a word with you."

"I have no intention of talking with that evil, vile demon."

Prous grinned and hit her hard enough to send her flying. Dazed, Queen Ciella was filled with determined rage and released her talons. As always happened when she was in grave danger, adrenaline flooded her body. Upset that she had gotten away from him, Ripkin charged in. Queen Ciella clipped the net with her talons and sent Prous flying into Ripkin. Free of the net, she fell toward the ground. Prous straightened himself and gave chase.

Queen Ciella realized that if she did not free herself from these two now, this would become a fool's errand. She saw the orange bow of the Causeway and leaped onto it. Prous dove to grab Queen Ciella and they collided, sending each of them flying off in a different direction.

Prous woke up at the feet of Stous.

"So what do I have here?" Stous said. "Prous, you have failed me." He raised his muscular leg to squash him.

Egosorous ran up to him. "Don't do that, Master. We still have a use for him."

"Ahh. Fine." Lowering his leg, Stous waved his deformed claw. "Get him out of here. But if he fails again, Egosorous, I'll hold you responsible!"

Egosorous leaned in and grabbed Prous. "You owe me."

"No, you can't be dead." Christopher looked into Artie's ashen eyes. He applied pressure to Artie's chest. "One, one thousand, two one thousand, three one thousand—hold on! Stay with me."

Reaching out, touching Christopher's shoulder, Paola whispered, "I believe he is past that point."

"No way am I giving up." Resuming, Christopher looked at Artie. "This is hard, but you must fight. You can do it."

Queen Ciella found herself in the Orange Realm. Flicking her hand, she disappeared and reappeared in the vault. She fell to her knees and saw the dagger sticking out of her side. She pulled the blade out gasping and collapsed. The last of the precious moments moved through the portal. *Artie has the will to fight; I have to get to the elixir.*

Artie looked up at Christopher. His eyes wavered and fluttered as he tried to say, "Thank you, leave me."

Christopher shook his head. "No, no," he said as one of his tears fell onto Artie's cheek.

Artie felt the hot tear and stirred.

Queen Ciella dragged herself across the floor of the vault and reached up for the pouch marked Angelic. It hit the ground and wobbled only to stop against the wall. The blood continued to streak the floor as she clawed her way to the wall. Queen Ciella grabbed the pouch and poured some on the wound and with a wave of her hand, she appeared next to Christopher. Their eyes met, all feelings and questions now answered.

"Step back." Queen Ciella uncorked the flask.

The aroma of Frankincense and Pachulia oil sent a message of comfort to everyone. She applied the elixir to his wound. As she worked the lotion into his skin, the colors of the Orange Realm swirled around him, faded, and took the bleeding wound with them. Artie opened his eyes and felt the injury that was no longer there.

"Queen Ciella!" he exclaimed, "how can I ever thank you? I thought I was a goner!"

Alone in his chamber, Stous ruminated over his battles, the loss of an eye, his missing horn and deformed claw. How could all this have happened? He sat quietly before realizing his sole triumph. With a quizzical look, he turned to see clutched in his slimy claw the one thing that would spell the doom for those two human creatures. The amulet.

The companions gathered around Artie, hugging him in disbelief. Everyone was both delighted and amazed by the power of Queen Ciella's elixir. Now, they were free to take a deep breath and enjoy the safety of Cloud Kingdom.

Leah and Christopher felt it first. They smiled and felt full of joy. They leaped into the air, fists raised high, and shouted, "We made it! And Qtrous is safe!"

"Yes," Artie added. "Fulfilling our oaths and duty. But for the goodness and kindness of old and new friends alike!"

Oda looked at Paola, each knowing that their mission wasn't entirely completed. They needed to find a way to reunite the souls and bodies of the children. Q and Lorous joined the celebration, grabbing Qtrous and asking him where he'd been.

"We've been waiting right here, worried silly!" they said in unison to a reply of laughter.

Artie smiled and laughed as well but took a step back when he realized something was missing. He reached under his shirt to look for the amulet. It was gone.

Artie kept quiet.

Christopher and Leah felt great about returning home, safe and sound after so much adventure.

At the dining room table, Mom leaned over and said, "We have a special dessert tonight."

"Oh, yeah? Why's that?" asked Dad.

"Well, your daughter did a good deed, and I thought we should celebrate."

"Indeed," said Dad. "So, spill it, girl. What did you do?"

Leah smiled. "Well, there were bullies on the bus, and they kept picking on this boy, Ben. I stopped them! I told them all to shut up, sit down, and leave him alone. You should have seen it!"

Father grinned and said, "Alright, that's my girl."

He looked over at Christopher as if to say, "That's how you handle bullies."

"Now, you need to go talk to these so-called bullies and straighten things out."

"I know, Dad," Leah smiled. "I already did."

Dad turned to Mom. "I thought about you when I flew over the house today."

"Why?" she asked.

"I saw the most beautiful rainbow arching over our house. It was strange. The blue part of the rainbow seemed like it was glowing bright as a neon sign. Weirdest rainbow I ever saw."

Christopher and Leah exchanged knowing glances and smiled.

"That is weird, Dad," said Christopher

"Yeah, darnedest thing. Now, who's ready for ice cream?"

"We are!" Christopher and Leah cried.

PART
FOUR

*"The road narrows the closer we get
to the end of our journey."*

PART

FOUR

"The road narrows the closer we get
to the end of our journey."

TABLE OF CONTENTS

—PART FOUR—

Chapter 1

—Dangerous Travels—

Christopher and Leah enjoyed their dessert downstairs and followed it up with some rest in front of the TV. They were tuned in to an animated show about a family lost on a tropical island, but neither of the children were paying attention.

"Let's go back upstairs," said Leah. "Our adventures are better than what's on TV anyway."

Christopher smiled and nodded and they bounded up the stairs to Christopher's room. They sat cross-legged on his bed to talk about their last trip to Cloud Kingdom.

"Christopher, I know Dad has been talking about sending you to military school." Christopher's face flushed with embarrassment as he turned away from her.

"Ever since those kids took my stuff, Dad thinks I'm

a coward."

"I'm sorry, Christopher, but Dad hasn't seen you in Cloud Kingdom fighting and protecting the young while leading the charge at times and saving my life from Stous's electric bolts. You have learned so much in such a short time."

"Well, he probably never will. Let's change the subject."

"I know. Next time Dad brings it up, I'll tell them how all those bullies are now afraid of you."

"That would be nice, but Dad won't believe you. I don't think he'll believe it until he sees it with his own eyes. I don't want to talk about it anymore. He'll just have to notice the difference in me for himself."

"Our last mission was sure crazy."

"I know," Christopher agreed, "but it was also a lot more dangerous than the first time we went. Now we have Stous's minions to worry about, especially what are left of Stous's super soldiers."

Leah frowned. "Now that they are surrounding the realms, we never know where they might show up,"

Christopher looked thoughtful for a moment. "I just

remembered. We don't even have our amulet! How are we going to get it back?"

Leah smiled. "I'm sure Artie will know. He knows everything."

Christopher nodded, "You can say that again."

"That means we'll need to ask Elephantous again to help us get back one more time. I hope he's not tired of flying us around."

Christopher chuckled. "Nah, he seems eager to help, but we'll wait until tomorrow to go back."

"Oh, that's right! Our friends are coming over soon!"

"We should start getting ready," Christopher said, jumping down from his bed.

Leah followed, smoothing out the sheets behind her. "It's too bad we can't bring our friends to Cloud Kingdom."

"Someday." Christopher grinned and then suddenly looked inspired. "Of course, we could always pretend we're there! When our friends come over, we can play a game outside and tell them all about the Cloud people and the Rainbow Causeway. They don't have to know we've been there."

Leah smiled. "They'll just think it's a make-believe game. At least we'll find out what other kids think about our crazy adventures."

Leah and Christopher high-fived and headed towards the stairs.

At the top step, Leah stopped short and grabbed her brother by the arm. "Wait," she whispered, "did you hear that?"

"No."

"It sounded like someone snickering," she added, looking back toward her room.

Christopher rolled his eyes. "You're hearing things. Let's go."

Leah crossed her arms and looked flatly at her brother. "The last time you said I was hearing things, a blue rainbow came into the room."

Christopher shrugged. "Good point. Go ahead. I'll check your room."

Christopher didn't bother to turn on the lights. He could see well enough thanks to moonlight shining through a crack in the curtains. Christopher trudged towards the door, he stopped suddenly. Something moved or he thought it did. Standing perfectly still, he listened as hard as he could. Nothing. The floor squeaked, *Is that what I heard? The floor squeaking? Maybe.* A million things ran through his mind. *Who could be in there? Was it a minion?*

Step by step, he cautiously moved closer to the door. His arm shook as he reached out to open it. He heard the eerie squealing noise of the door opening. That noise sent shivers up his spine filling him with fear. He braced himself, and started to peek around the door when he heard a loud voice say, "Hurry up!" Christopher jumped, and his heart began to race. Bounding down the stairs, Christopher yelled, "I'm coming."

In the shadows of the closet, Rhinosorous blinked his eyes and returned his dagger to its sheath.

Christopher grinned as he reached Leah. "See, no rainbows this time."

Chapter 2

-New Ally-

The drawbridge at the main gate of Cloud Kingdom was pulled shut, sealing off the entrance to the vast Cloud City beyond. No cloud creatures could be seen along the top of the walls. Arriving at the drawbridge after his long journey, Artie found himself face to face with a stranger. Slowly they circled each other, their eyes locked, hands raised as if both were ready to strike at any second.

Despite the standoff, Artie smiled in his usual way. "What brings you here, my friend?" he asked without dropping his trademark grin.

The other creature seemed out of place among the clouds as if from another realm. It was tall, much taller than the elf, and had huge wings that when unfurled made the drawbridge gate disappear. The creature's most noteworthy trait was the pair of identical heads on its shoulders, each one of them staring angrily at Artie.

The one on the left answered his question. "I am Dragonfly. I come from the realm of Purple Paradise."

Artie couldn't help but notice how strangely beautiful Dragonfly was, even holding a sword and glaring at him as she was. The entire creature was a beautiful lavender color and when she moved, her tough alligator skin glittered. It gave the appearance of sparkling diamonds.

The head that had spoken bore large eyes with wondrously long eyelashes. The other head, Artie noted, seemed far less friendly; it sized him up, taking in his full measure as if deciding how to attack.

The second, calculating head spoke next. "I will have you for my footstool, you foolish imp! Now leave me to my business!" While Dragonfly's words were spoken in a sing-song voice, the angrier head made them sound like cuts from a sharp knife.

Artie looked up at both heads and smiled wide. "Do your worst, friend. I just won't let someone as big as you run around the kingdom waving a sword."

"I am not your friend, you imp! And that thing you are doing is getting old, so, you'd better *can it*!" With a piercing screech, Dragonfly struck out and pinned Artie to the ground.

Finding himself face to face with the creature, Artie asked, "What am I doing that's getting old?"

With a wave of his hand, Dragonfly flipped onto her back, and Artie stood on her armored stomach. He cracked his knuckles, and a small flurry of magic dust sparkled down from his hands.

Dragonfly hissed. "Calling me your friend. And that constant, insidious smile of yours!"

"Well," Artie replied, "your name-calling is getting old. It's really not needed."

"Ah, is that right?" screamed Dragonfly.

With a push, Artie flew away. A few deft somersaults carried him head over heels, but he managed to land upright and ready. "You know I'm not an imp, right?"

"I will call you whatever I please, imp!"

"I don't think so, Dragonfly, especially in this realm. If you haven't noticed by now, my powers are quite strong here."

"And what realm is this that's so special they must

close their gates to me and send imps to fight me at the drawbridge?" asked Dragonfly.

"Before you learn the answer," Artie chuckled, "you must learn some manners."

"And I supposed you're going to teach me," Dragonfly laughed as she stood to her full height, towering over Artie. She spread her massive purple wings and pointed the tip of her shining sword directly towards the elf.

He bowed as if to say *bring it on.* "That's right. My name is Artie. Artie, the Elf."

With a fierce roar, Dragonfly charged toward Artie. Waiting until the last possible second, Artie stepped aside, causing the creature to smack headfirst into the drawbridge. Dragonfly looked dizzy as she stumbled backward.

Artie rubbed his hands together in a cloud of golden sparkles and floated casually to the same height as Dragonfly's heads. He smiled at her. "Care to try that again?"

With a *swoosh* and a growl, Dragonfly sliced her sword through the air. The blade should have cut the tiny elf to pieces, but by the time she swung round, Artie was gone.

"Now, about those manners," Artie continued.

The surprised Dragonfly pointed her heads in every direction trying to spot the elf. Without warning, she was thrown to the ground by a shower of golden sparks and landed on her backside with a thud. She struggled to get up, ready to lash out at the maddening elf but found herself stuck to the ground.

"Let me up!" she screamed as Artie floated toward her.

Artie cocked his head curiously. "I hope I'm not rude, but I noticed that one of your heads is much nicer than the other. Two heads, two personalities...does that mean you have two names?"

"I said LET ME UP!" Dragonfly shrieked, still struggling against Artie's invisible bonds.

Artie sighed. "I'd much rather talk to the nicer of the two of you. What is it that has you so angry?"

Dragonfly appeared to finally give up her struggle. Sinking back slightly, she began to explain in a calm monotone. "I made my way through a dozen realms before finding this one. Not one of them was kind or welcoming. Every realm was a fight and I can't trust someone who simply floats about smiling at me."

Artie frowned. "I'm sorry to hear about your bad fortune, but this realm is peaceful. No one here wants to harm you."

Dragonfly sighed. "I suppose not, but you've trapped me here like a winged bird. I guess if you'd wanted to end me, you could have done so already."

Artie laughed and released his magical bonds. He chuckled. "I would never. Although you had me second guessing myself when you started waving that giant sword around!"

To Artie's surprise, both of Dragonfly's heads seemed to give him a half a smile as he helped her to her feet. Still floating in the air in front of her, he grinned. "Now can we resolve to be friends?"

"Certainly. It's good to finally meet someone who doesn't want to battle. And to answer your question, I do have two true names. Once known by a friend we may be called upon by name to help in any situation anytime anywhere." Dragonfly's left head spoke first, batting her long lashes. "I am Gracie." Then the second head spoke, this time with much less anger. "And I am Giuliana."

Artie smiled and bowed in mid-air. "It's a pleasure to—"

Suddenly the air around them exploded with a wave of black smoke and thunder and lighting. Artie fell straight to the ground and even the giant Dragonfly staggered to her knees, both faces wincing from the blast.

"What was that?" hissed Dragonfly. "Did you just attack me after all that nonsense about peace and friendship?"

Artie got to his feet, shaking his head to fight the ringing in his ears. "That would have been a lousy attack if I had launched it," he said slyly. "I think it did more harm to me than to you."

Dragonfly huffed and then began scanning the horizon for attackers, her sword at the ready.

"And this was my favorite coat." Artie frowned, holding what remained of a sleeve, ripped and burned from the thundering blast.

"You'll be mourning more than the loss of your coat if you don't get it together, Artie the Elf!" Dragonfly shouted. "Help me look for the enemy before they strike once more!"

Artie looked up as if suddenly recovering from the shock. "Wait," he said. "I'm fairly sure I know who caused that cloudburst, and if I'm right, they've scurried off rather than facing an actual battle with us."

Dragonfly grinned. "Then whoever they are, they're wise."

"Was the last realm you were in, before you came here, full of dark clouds? Lots of thunder and rumbling?"

"Yes," nodded Dragonfly. "The creatures seemed to want to fight each other as much as they wanted to fight me."

"Stratocloudous," Artie said. "Some of the creatures must have followed you here, which makes me wonder how you were able to get out of their realm in the first place."

Dragonfly took one last look around. Satisfied that their attackers had fled, she sheathed her sword. "Well, I know a lot of secrets when it comes to traveling. As I said, I've been through dozens of realms over the course of many, many years."

"Interesting," said Artie. "I really must know more about—"

"Whatever you must know will have to wait," Dragonfly interrupted. "You say that I've brought enemies into your realm, and therefore I must take care of them. I will return."

"Wait! You have done enough!"

Before Artie could finish, Dragonfly wrapped herself in her wings and began to spin. Faster and faster, she spun creating a tiny light, until Artie could hardly see her at all. When the light blinked off, Dragonfly disappeared.

Chapter 3

-*A Surprise Visit*-

"Our friends really liked our imaginary version of Cloud Kingdom," Christopher said as they climbed the steps.

"Yeah, they sure did," agreed Leah. "I'll bet they'd really love to visit the real one!"

Christopher chuckled. "Of course they would. Who wouldn't?"

After saying their prayers and tucking in Leah and Christopher, their parents went back downstairs as they usually did. They'd been downstairs for some time when Leah headed into Christopher's room.

"Are you asleep yet, Christopher?"

"Nope, just reading," was the reply from the hill of blankets on Christopher's bed. The shimmer of his night light surrounded his bed.

"Good," said Leah, sitting on the edge of the bed. "I

was just thinking…"

Suddenly, something lit up the room as if the sun had appeared above their heads. They gaped open-mouthed at the sheet of white light that covered the ceiling. The light *sizzled, sparkled,* and began to swirl. Seconds later, a jagged black crack with a red edge appeared and split the ceiling. A ripping noise echoed through the room as the fissure widened, and both Christopher and Leah gasped when a hand reached through the opening. The claw glinted with the remains of scimitar-like talons.

"It can't be…" whispered Leah, shaking at the sight.

Christopher pointed at something glinting in the light. "Look!"

It was a golden amulet hanging from a chain around the twisted, bloodied claw.

"That's the amulet!" Leah shouted.

Both kids flattened themselves on the bed in a panic as the black, blood-stained claw darted towards them. Leah shut her eyes and let out a squeal, but a second went by, and all she could see was the room returning to darkness.

"It's gone," whispered Christopher.

The room was entirely back to normal, except for a strange stain on the floor next to the bed. The light was gone, and more importantly, so was the claw. Leah heaved a sigh of relief and heard her brother do the same. In the closet next door, Rhinosorous quivered as he felt the presence of Stous.

"Arrrgh, almost!" screamed Stous as the light dissipated.

Far away from the darkened bedrooms of the children, in one of the many realms beyond, a wounded Egosorous stumbled through a field of jagged clouds.

"Outcast from Stratocloudous!" he growled to himself. "And all thanks to Rhinosorous, the betrayer!"

Egosorous tripped, barely managing to break his fall as he landed on the ground with a grunt.

"I'll get you for this," he groaned. "And I will see Stous fall."

Egosorous could feel the weakness in his bones as darkness crept in. His vision became blurry, but he could still see a creature stepping out of the shadows toward him, and he could make out the jagged teeth of its smile.

"Well, well, what do we have here?" the creature said. "A newcomer to the realm of mirrored clouds?"

The last thing Egosorous heard before blacking out was the creature laughing, followed by a few sharper words.

"Welcome to Pridosorous."

Chapter 4

–*Dragonfly Meets Queen Ciella*–

Artie frowned as Dragonfly disappeared, apparently off to hunt any of Stous's minions that had followed her into the realm of the cloud folk. The elf felt something was amiss and terribly wrong throughout the realms. With a resigned sigh, he clapped his hands together to summon his magic flying carpet, Aero.

Artie climbed aboard. "Let's take a ride to the Orange Kingdom."

Aero curled upward and gestured with its tassels.

"No," Artie shook his head. "We won't need Elephantous to come with us. I have a feeling he'll be needed elsewhere very soon."

Aero nodded his flaps and zoomed off toward the realm of the Orange Kingdom, home to Queen Ciella. Artie and Aero arrived at their destination several hours later. The elf was disappointed and worried by the lack of rainbows on the way, as it meant they could not speed up their journey. It was unusual to travel that far without seeing at least one rainbow and it confirmed his fears that something was amiss in the realms.

Upon arriving in Orange Kingdom, Artie guided Aero toward Queen Ciella's palace. He was shocked to be suddenly reunited with Dragonfly there.

"Dragonfly!" he exclaimed, pulling Aero to a stop in front of a huge cage where the tall, beautiful creature was unhappily trapped behind bars.

"Did you come uninvited to this realm, too?" Artie chuckled. "I thought you would have learned your lesson about knocking on someone's door with a sword in your hand."

"That isn't what happened at all," the kinder head of Gracie said in her sing-song voice.

"Unlock the latch!" growled Giuliana, the head that was still struggling with Artie's earlier lesson on good manners.

"I can't do that," said Artie, "but I do know someone

in this realm that could."

"Well, unless it's the queen, we're out of luck. I doubt it will help," hissed Giuliana.

Artie chuckled. "Ha! Well…you're in luck."

As if summoned by the words, a beautiful portal appeared beside the cage. Queen Ciella floated through with a welcoming smile for Artie. "Good to see you, my friend. Has my new guest been bothering you? One of her heads can be quite rude."

Giuliana said, rattling her cage. "I'd bow, your majesty, but there isn't enough room in this stinking cage. Is this how you treat guests?"

Queen Ciella nodded toward Dragonfly. "Well, maybe an uninvited guest."

"I actually know Dragonfly," said Artie, trying to stop any harsher words. "How did she end up being caged?"

"My soldiers found a handful of Stous's minions at the borders of the kingdom," the queen explained. "This creature was among them, armed with a sword and a disrespectful tongue."

"I've told you," Dragonfly cut in, "I was hunting the

same minions. The elf can tell you all about it."

Artie nodded. "She's telling the truth. She was in Cloud Kingdom when we faced their attack together." He decided to leave out the part about how Dragonfly led Stous's minions into Cloud Kingdom in the first place.

Queen Ciella looked thoughtful for a moment, and then the bars disintegrated with a wave of her hand. "You must behave in my kingdom," added the queen before allowing Dragonfly to continue speaking.

"Much better. As I was saying." Dragonfly said.

Queen Ciella and Artie gave her a stern nod.

The tall, winged creature nodded sullenly and said, "There's something more worrisome than Stous's minions. As I told the elf, I've been traveling through the realms for some time. Recently, I've seen whole cities abandoned—thousands of cloud folk at a time migrating away from them."

"Hmm, that is unusual," said Artie.

"Yes," Dragonfly continued, "and it has made it possible for Stous's minions to take up residence in the cities the cloud folk have left behind. Large groups of

Stous's minions are moving in and taking over the gates and borders of the realms."

"We will need to talk to Oda and Paola to see if more of their children are missing besides the ones being held in the cage fields on Tundrasorous," Artie said.

Chapter 5

-New Threats-

"So Stous is gaining control of the ways in and out of the realms. This cannot be allowed!" exclaimed Queen Ciella.

Artie frowned. "I worry that they may have control of the Rainbow Causeway as well. I'm not sure, but I haven't seen many rainbows lately, and that's not a good sign."

Queen Ciella agreed with a forlorn nod.

"In fact," Artie went on, "the whole reason I traveled here was to see if you had any information on what is happening."

"I have been dealing with the important business of the Evil Eight since we left Tundrasorous," she said, "but I can assure you that the Orange Kingdom is secure."

The solemn tone of the conversation suddenly broke as a sizzling *pop* echoed through the air. Dragonfly reached for the sword that was no longer at her side, and Artie sprang into readiness. He relaxed when he heard the trumpeting of Elephantous from outside the palace.

"Look who it is!" he said, laughing as Christopher and Leah came running in through the gates.

Both children looked panicked, and they were talking so fast that Artie couldn't understand a word.

"Okay," he interrupted, "calm down! One at a time."

Leah nodded to her brother and waved him forward.

"Alright," said Christopher, "this is what happened."

He quickly explained the wall of light and the claw that appeared through the crack within. He also told of the amulet wrapped around the claw and the bloodstain that was left behind when the light disappeared.

"Some kind of portal," Artie said. "Stous is trying to get at you in your own realm, and it looks like he's using the amulet to track you."

"So, Stous is able to breach realms and travel as he wills?" Queen Ciella asked.

"No," said a familiar voice from the entrance of the

palace.

All heads turned to see Lord Mason of the Rainbow Causeway, furrowing his colorful golden wings behind him as he entered with purpose.

"I'm sorry to arrive unannounced, but I bring news," he continued. "Stous grows in power, and I've been forced to secure the Rainbow Causeway. As of now, he doesn't control it, and I aim to keep it that way."

Artie felt immediate relief. It was a far less grim explanation for the lack of rainbows.

"For now, Stous has only a basic command of portals. From the spell book he had stolen from the Purple Paradise realm, he learned incantations to open portals, but he still can't travel through them. His minions can, of course, but he's been cursed since the first realm wars never to leave Stratocloudous. An angel of God came to the once Utopia realm and snatched up Stous and threw him into Stratocloudous and tethered him to the core of the realm with a magic ankle bracelet."

"He has almost no power with portals," Artie said thoughtfully, "and yet he used the power to try to travel to Leah and Christopher."

"Why couldn't he just escape Stratocloudous by going to one of the closer realms?" asked Dragonfly. "Anywhere would be better than there."

"Because he wants these two children more than anything else," Lord Mason said, nodding toward Christopher and Leah.

"He wants to ruin our plans to create a relationship between their realm and our own," Queen Ciella said.

"Let's not forget he's also trying to steal the souls of children in other realms," Artie interjected.

"What do you mean?" asked Christopher.

"We've been trying to create a permanent bridge between your world and Cloud Kingdom," explained Queen Ciella. "A way to bring all children through to enjoy the realms, just as you have. Stous is positioning himself to steal dreams and the souls of young children to turn them into minions so that Cloud Kingdom will be populated by his servants, all willing to do his bidding."

"We must stop Stous!" Leah exclaimed.

"You're absolutely right," said Artie.

"There's something more," Lord Mason continued.

"The immediate problem we face is that the gateway to the realm of children has been closed. Strange enough, it has been closed from the children's side."

"Impossible!" exclaimed Artie. "How can that be?"

Christopher and Leah shared a worried look.

"How will we get home?" Christopher asked.

"With your realm closed," replied Lord Mason, "you can't go home."

Leah gasped and Christopher's eyes turned to saucers.

Artie floated over to comfort them. "We will get you home, somehow. There's always a way. However, for now, we must stop Stous from crossing over to the other realms. I want to introduce you to someone. This is Dragonfly. Dragonfly, this is Captain Christopher and Commander Leah."

Leah bowed, as did Dragonfly. Christopher's left eyebrow went up as he heard the creature's familiar name.

"I believe we have a mutual friend," Christopher said.

All who were present turned to Christopher with puzzled looks.

"I have a message for you, Dragonfly," Christopher said.

Dragonfly bent down, and Christopher got between both heads as they leaned in to hear Christopher relay Griseous message.

Without hesitation, Dragonfly took a couple of paces toward the center of the room, covered herself in her wings, and spun out of the castle. The Council looked on with disbelief.

As the confused murmurs died out, Queen Ciella asked, "What did you tell her?"

"Yeah, Christopher, how do you know her, and I don't?" Leah insisted.

Before Christopher could answer, there was a loud *swoosh*. Greicius landed in the middle of the group with Dragonfly right behind.

"Christopher, thank you for keeping your word," Greicius yelled.

The Council looked around to see the source of the voice, but all they could see was an old, charred rock.

"I want you to meet someone," Dragonfly said pointing

to Greicius.

"Who is that?" the Council members asked in unison.

"Hi, my name is Greicius, and I am not a 'that' or and 'it,'" the rock said.

"Greicius is a charr-asteroid who saved my life many years ago. I had to return the favor," Dragonfly said.

"He also helped me get out of that star tunnel on my first trip to Cloud Kingdom," Christopher said.

"Welcome," the Council said.

"Thank you," Greicius replied. "Now it's been a long time, and I must get back to my home star."

With that, there was a rumble, a *swoosh*, and Greicius was gone.

Artie chuckled. "Do all your friends come and go so fast without a hello or good-bye?"

With one head wagging left to right and the other head nodding, Dragonfly laughed too.

"Well, back to business," said Queen Ciella.

Through all of this, Dragonfly wasn't ready to share

her knowledge, but she knew there was a way to get the children home. She had seen a creature called Rhinosorous cross over into the children's realm, which meant that it was possible.

Egosorous thought the realm he'd landed in was anything but perfect. Strangely, the creature that had found him staggering before he blacked out did not agree. When he woke, the creature had introduced himself as General Prous in Stous's army, and now he was eagerly describing just how perfect his realm was.

"Yes, I have seen you but mostly on the battlefield," Egosorous replied.

"The Realm of Mirrored Clouds known as Pridosorous is ideal in every way," he said, grinning ear to ear and showing every one of his teeth. "Everything one might need is right there. It's beautiful thunder and clashing clouds perform all the time. It's like music!"

Egosorous nodded along. In a way, the realm reminded him a bit of Stratocloudous; it wasn't really the same, but it would do. He was a perfect creature, and he would hatch the ideal plan to get revenge on Stous and Rhinosorous.

If nothing else, this realm would be the picture-perfect place to prepare his attack.

Pridosorous was extremely beautiful outside and very wicked on the inside. Creatures that entered his realm would only think of something beautiful, and it would appear as part of the countless web of mazes. The inner core was ruled by Prous and his evil energy that transformed the clouds to what his prey wanted.

"So Stous has learned to open portals? He's not doing it very well," Leah said.

"That's right," Lord Mason explained. "He somehow got his claws on a stolen book from the realm of Purple Paradise that contains all of the spells that he needs. He's just not skilled enough to use all of them."

"Depending on how long he's had the book, he may have had plenty of time to practice," said Queen Ciella.

"I know the book you're speaking of," Dragonfly said. "Our entire realm knows of its theft. It occurred an exceptionally long time ago, as far back as Stous's exile from the realms."

"So, he may have had this book since he was first sent to Stratocloudous?" Artie asked.

Dragonfly shrugged. "Perhaps."

Chapter 6

-Dragonfly Speaks Up-

The room fell silent for a long moment before Dragonfly lowered her heads and let out a long sigh. "It humbles me to say this," she said. "I'm not one to ask for help but I'm also not one to keep secrets from friends, and I've seen that each of you share the same goal I do."

"Yes, of course, we do." Artie said. "What is it you must share?"

"A creature, one of Stous's minions, has traveled to the children's realm. From what I can tell from tracking him, he's still there. He's most likely stuck there now after the passage to the children's realm was sealed."

Christopher and Leah's mother began her nightly ritual of washing the dishes, carefully scrubbing each one before placing it in the dishwasher. She was startled when a loud thud echoed through the house from upstairs.

"Hey, kids!" she yelled up at the ceiling, "Stop horsing around up there!"

She would have been even more startled to know that it wasn't her children that had made the noise, but Rhinosorous, now frozen in his tracks from the sound of her voice.

"So Rhinosorous is in the children's realm?" Artie frowned at Dragonfly. "What else aren't you telling us?"

"A lot," snickered Giuliana, the head on her right shoulder.

"Stop that teasing right now," snapped the other politer head belonging to Gracie. "This is serious business!"

"Indeed, it is." Queen Ciella scowled. "Would you care to enlighten us on everything else you know?"

Dragonfly hesitated for a moment and then tears began to stream down from all four of her eyes. "Forgive me," she said, choking back the tears. "It has been a long and hard journey for us."

"It's all right," said Leah in a comforting tone. "You can tell us."

"The spell book you're speaking of, the one that Stous is using to open portals—well, I'm not just familiar with it...I've been tasked with getting it back," Dragonfly continued. "I've been traveling through the realms for as long as it takes the sun to travel across the realms—all the while in search of this precious book."

Queen Ciella looked amazed. "That's an exceedingly long time. Generations would have passed in Elvin time. Hundreds of years."

"Yes," said Dragonfly. "And in all that time, I've learned much about the realms. Much that will be useful to you in taking Stous down forever."

"This is welcome news," said Lord Mason. "I'm eager to hear more, especially regarding how much time it will take Stous to learn the spells from the book."

"Well," Dragonfly mused, "the children claim he was able to open a portal large enough to reach his claw through. It will take him much more skill to travel between realms, but he's much closer than he's ever been."

"Then there's no time to waste," Queen Ciella stated. "We must finish him and that special squad before he becomes more powerful. Once we've retrieved the book, Dragonfly, your age long quest will finally be at an end."

For the first time since meeting her new friends, both of Dragonfly's heads smiled.

"The special cloud games are planned this weekend and we must allow the cloud people to enjoy them," said Artie. "With all the uprooting and shifts of populations, their lives have been disrupted enough. They'll need something positive to dwell on."

Queen Ciella spoke up. "I have a few suggestions for you. I believe Oda and Paola can help upgrade the games' security and find out if there are any other fields of cages that Stous has been using."

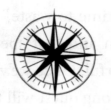

Chapter 7

- The Games -

The courtyard of Cloud Kingdom's huge castle buzzed with excitement. Hundreds of cloud people gathered amid music and waving banners. The balloons that floated through the air were every color of the rainbow. Young cloud folk jumped to catch them as they drifted by. Huge tents were set up, each with a cloud vendor selling boots, belts, hats, and other fancy wares. Other shelters had delicious foods and the smells of cottony cloud candy, and puffy cloudcorn wafted through the crowd.

Hundreds of different creatures milled about, all present for the yearly Cloudasorous games. While Stous had displaced many with his takeover of the other realms, the downtrodden joined along just the same. The games were the perfect distraction from the growing chaos beyond the walls.

A horn trumpeted to signal the start of the games. Artie stood and got the courtyard's attention. "Please listen. As you know, earlier this year we lost two close friends and great soldiers of the realm to the Evil Eight as they tried to protect the castle. To all their families and friends, I say let's honor their memories with our own bravery and love for one another." Artie raised his arms and the crowd yelled "Here! Here!" and cheered for their two fallen comrades, Clous and Mars.

The games began with the Cloud Funnel Race, in which participants rode whirling clouds that looked like miniature tornadoes. The challenge was to both ride fast and race, jump, and steer without breaking the funnel.

The Float and Grab would follow this, a favorite game of Artie's friends Q and Lorous. In this game, the players jumped on a whirling cloud as it floated around a hanging rope full of candy clouds; the winner was whoever grabbed the most candy before falling off their cloud. Q and Lorous were both extremely good at this game and were already favored as the champions.

Of course, the most beloved and anticipated event at the games was the Dinosorous Race. When the race began, two lines of dinosorous would face off and clash heads until one remained standing. The remaining dinosorous would then chase a fluffy, long-eared rabbisorous before catching it. If the dinosorous weren't too dizzy at this point, it would then run to the finish line and climb the cloud slide—a challenge because the steps of the slide were continually moving and shifting. Each step became a hazard and if you missed one you found yourself back at the starting line. While the excitement and fun built in the courtyard, the future of the realms were being decided in the castle above.

Chapter 8

– *The Council* –

As the new Council took roll call, the members raised their hands as their names were called: Queen Ciella, Artie, Lord Mason, Dragonfly, Commander Leah, Captain Christopher, Ola, and Paola. After this, Queen Ciella called for order. Just as everyone was taking a seat at a large, round table, a familiar face ran through the door. Liam, the librarian, bowed to the Council and took the remaining seat.

"Thank you for joining us on such short notice," Queen Ciella said. "Let us begin."

Lord Mason cleared his throat and began. "As we all know, Stous's minions are taking over many of the realms and stealing increasingly more souls. He is becoming too powerful, and we're here to figure out how to stop him before he's able to escape Stratocloudous."

Lord Mason looked over at Liam. "You may not have been informed, but Leah and Christopher have reported that Stous has already begun creating portals using a long-lost spell book from the Purple Paradise realm. His portals are small and weak, but his power grows."

"There's also the matter of Stous's minion Rhinosorous traveling to the children's realm," added Queen Ciella. "He is the only one so far that has made it that far and is now trapped."

Liam nodded along as he took in this new information.

Lord Mason continued. "You may already be aware that I've been building a branch of the Rainbow Causeway to the children's realm so that others like Leah and Christopher can come through to enjoy Cloud Kingdom. However, these latest problems could delay building the connection."

At this, Leah and Christopher both looked sad.

"I see," said Liam. "Much has happened while I have been buried in my books."

"Indeed," said Queen Ciella, "but we've been fortunate enough to gain a new warrior. Bowing slightly toward Dragonfly, she said, "Dragonfly is from the realm of Purple Paradise. For those of us who are not familiar with this realm, it is inhabited by every type of creature who dabbles in magic. Also, it's the place to buy and sell all things magical, including spells. Dragonfly has seen more of the realms than any of us, and has pledged to take the spell book from Stous and end his plans."

Dragonfly nodded with a stern thrust of her heads. "I believe I can be of much help in catching Stous and his minions. There are unusual ways to travel the realms, including the children's realm. Ways that only I know."

"Excellent," said Queen Ciella. "I'm certain that will be useful. For now, we must resolve our plan to confront Stous."

"Agreed," said Lord Mason. "I suggest that we begin by sending spies throughout the realms to gather as much information as possible. We can't act any further until we're sure of Stous's exact location."

"Yes, and even though we know he's somewhere in Stratocloudous," said Artie, "we should plan to confront him in another realm."

"A good point," nodded Queen Ciella. "He will be most powerful in his own realm. And we must also assume that he may learn how to travel to a new realm at any time."

"And the last step of the plan?" asked Liam.

"To face Stous," said Dragonfly. "And take care of him for the last time."

Everyone at the table nodded.

"Captain Christopher and I will gladly spy for you," Leah volunteered.

"Your eagerness is noted," smiled Queen Ciella, "but it would be far too dangerous. Every one of Stous's minions is looking for you, and you do stand out in a crowd."

"I think Dragonfly would be the best suited for spying as she has been in and out of all the realms," Lord Mason said.

"I agree," said Queen Ciella. "She has been traveling the realms unnoticed for centuries. There could be none better."

Without a word, Dragonfly nodded and stood from her chair. With a flourish and a whirling spin, she disappeared from the room.

"That one will be an asset to the realms one day," said Queen Ciella, "once she learns to control her emotions and passions."

Artie grinned. "You should have seen her when I met her."

"Ah, yes," smiled the queen. "Artie, you and the children should scour the realms for a place to do battle with Stous. Choose somewhere that gives us the greatest advantage. Meet us back here when the third cloud from the sun moves over Cloud Kingdom."

"We're on it," said Artie, smiling to the siblings.

"Liam, you will stay behind with Lord Mason and me to form the battle plan. We must be sure that nothing is left to chance."

"Oda and Paola, I will leave Elephantous with you so you may do some recon on Stous's minions. Continue to look for more cage fields that we don't know of yet. We can meet back here in a fortnight," said Artie with a bow.

Summoning Aero, he and the siblings climbed on board to begin scouting.

Chapter 9

-Valley of Distrust-

As Dragonfly whirled she saw the council chamber disappear, her eyes resting on large, black clouds when she came to a stop. "Stratocloudous," she said to herself. "I hate this place."

Unfurling her wings, she glided silently through the rocks and crude, back alleys, and black buildings built from thunderclouds. She would find Stous and that would mean finding the book that she'd been seeking for centuries. She moved with haste, feeling drawn toward a deep crevice in the black clouds.

"The Valley of Distrust," she whispered. "A suitable place, if any."

She knew it from her past journeys. The valley was a place where all friendship fell apart as if through dark magic. Within it, no one could feel loyalty, trust, or companionship. It was a place of pure ugliness. It was only moments after entering the valley that Dragonfly felt the shock of an energy bolt flying near her head. She dodged swiftly as another buzzed through where she had been.

"Stous's minions!" shouted Gracie from the left shoulder.

"It gets worse," replied Giuliana, "there's Stous!"

She pointed just in time for Gracie to see Stous firing a bolt of energy toward them. Giuliana raised their shield to block most of the strike but shuddered as part of an energy bolt spell dashed through her own head. Strangely, it didn't hurt and Gracie didn't even notice.

"Let's get out of here!" both heads said in unison, folding their wings and spinning. An instant later, Dragonfly left the valley, leaving Stous and a handful of his minions behind.

"Stay put," said Stous, walking toward the place where Dragonfly had been. Without warning, he turned and fired a shock of energy into his own minions, disintegrating them where they stood. "Ha!" He chuckled. "One should never forget that they're in the Valley of Distrust!" He then opened his claw, revealing a bright, glowing ball of light. Inside, he could see the head of the flying creature that he'd just attacked. "Wonderful! My spell landed on one of Dragonfly's heads at least."

He grinned as a voice came through the glowing ball: "We have to go back! We have to go get the book!" Gracie said.

Stous's wicked smile grew even broader. "What a useful spell, indeed. I can hear what you hear and see what you see." Stous laughed, a movement that exposed his jagged teeth and also showed his delirium. "I wonder what else I can do to you now."

Since exiled from Stratocloudous, Egosorous had little magic left—enough to fly but not much else. Planning his revenge against Stous, Egosorous summoned up whatever magic he had left and turned himself into an apparition. Wisping down to Stratocloudous, he found himself in the Valley of Distrust. Egosorous poked his head around the cloud that gave him cover. Only the red veins in his eyes and the dripping saliva from his teeth were visible. Drawing back his head, he snickered to himself, "I can almost taste my revenge." He sat back watching Stous, waiting for the right moment.

Stous taunted his minions. "Watch and learn my minions." He raised his arms up and out and began reciting an incantation. Bringing his arms midway down with palms facing each other, the electricity built, small at first until it became a ball of pure electricity. "Go find my precious target and be true only to me," Stous cried out.

Egosorous created a ghost image of what had just taken place, including the creation of the spell, the casting of the incantation on Giuliana, and finally the killing of his own minion. He sent it off to Artie. Egosorous laughed and thought to himself, *That should weaken or destroy Stous.* Egosorous knew that Artie was clever enough to figure out who sent the ghost images. He also knew that the elf would understand that Egosorous wanted an ally to help take Stous down.

Chapter 10

The Plan

"Up ahead is Pridosorous," said Artie as Aero flew them toward the border. "It should serve as a perfect battleground."

Leah squinted at the horizon as the realm drew closer. "I don't see anything but a huge wall of clouds," she said.

Artie smiled. "That's what makes Pridosorous so ideal. It's really a huge maze of cloud walls. Once inside, every corner is a mystery. One turn could lead you to a scorching desert; the next, a shining cloud city, as splendid as any work of art." Guiding Aero down toward an entrance in the cloud wall, Artie added, "Here, let me show you."

They flew through long corridors of clouds, and it was precisely as Artie had said. Jungles of cloud trees down one bend, a sparkling lake covered in ice around the next. What amazed the siblings the most was the sky. Everything around them was mirrored above.

"That's how it is in this realm," explained Artie as he noticed them looking up. "All outward beauty in this realm is doubled, but the evil inside is hidden."

"What kind of evil?" asked Christopher. "This place seems like a paradise."

"The evil is well hidden," said Artie, pointing to a strange funnel of clouds ahead. "Just watch."

As they approached the funnel of clouds, it began to take on the shape of a face. It was disfigured and oddly shaped, with drooping eyes and jagged teeth that jutted in many directions—a deformed creature imprisoned in the walls.

"See. This realm may seem beautiful on the surface, but it could just as well swallow you up."

"It seems like a bad place to face Stous," said Christopher.

"Don't worry. I have a plan that will give us a huge advantage here. Now let's get out of this maze before we get lost."

As they sped back toward Cloud Kingdom, Artie sat in the front contemplating the strange message he had received. Thinking he knew who had sent it helped him envision different scenarios for the coming battle.

"We've returned," Artie announced as they stepped into the council chamber.

Queen Ciella and Lord Mason were draped over large battle maps and piles of Liam's scrolls but turned their attention to Artie. Liam himself didn't move as his nose was buried in a thick book on the table.

"You're incredibly early," said the queen. "How did your recon mission go? Just as well," she said without giving Artie a chance to answer. "We have truly little time to waste, and Lord Mason has been accommodating in arranging the battle plan. I trust you have found a suitable realm?"

Artie smiled. "Yes, Pridosorous."

"You're joking," Lord Mason grunted. "That place is devious and full of traps."

"That's exactly why we should use it. I have a few ideas for making it well-suited for our plans." Artie extended his hand to Christopher. "Here, let me see the remaining amulet for a moment."

Leah took the amulet from her pocket and handed it to her brother, who passed it along to Artie.

"Just needs a bit of tuning," the elf said, holding the amulet up to the light. He whispered into the amulet, "Whoever holds this amulet and speaks the words shall bring the other half, making the amulet whole again. Let the worthiness of the holder determine the true heir to its power and magic." Artie smiled and handed the amulet back to Leah. "There," he grinned. "Now when we are ready to put our plan in motion, this will bring Stous right to us. Assuming he still has the other half of the amulet, of course."

"Knowing Stous, it never leaves his claw," said Queen Ciella.

"For the next part, I will need Dragonfly. I suppose we'll need to wait a fortnight for her return."

"Not at all," said Queen Ciella. "She too arrived early." She nodded to her emissary and he took his leave to retrieve Dragonfly.

"Ah," Artie said. "Wonderful! It seems like good luck

is finally coming our way."

Moments later, Queen Ciella's emissary returned with Dragonfly close behind.

"Glad to see you found Stous so quickly," said Artie. "Now I need a favor." Artie floated up to Gracie's head on the left shoulder and began whispering.

"Hey!" said Giuliana from the right, "What am I, an orphan? What's going on?"

Gracie turned and repeated Artie's request: "We need to use our knowledge of the realm and our magic to create a map of Pridosorous."

"That's an odd place to want to go," snickered Giuliana, "but a map is a useful thing to have there."

Back in Stratocloudous, Stous listened through his glowing orb. "So, they're going to Pridosorous, eh?" he growled. "Well, thanks to my spell, I can help make their little map. A bit of mind control through my Dragonfly pet will change it just enough to get them lost forever in that maze!" Stous considered his plan for a moment. "I'll also make sure plenty of my minions are waiting inside to split their skulls!"

"Liam," Artie called out.

The librarian finally lifted his eyes from his book. "Artie!" he smiled. "When did you get back?"

Artie sighed and continued, "I need your help with something. We're going to Pridosorous. We have a way to get Stous there, and we're working on a map. I just need a spell that will keep us from getting lost in case there are problems with the map."

Liam nodded. "Yes, I suppose a map is only half of the solution. Things can change in that maze, and the routes aren't always the same."

"Do you know anything that will help?"

"There is a true direction spell that can keep you from getting lost as long as you know your destination," Liam said. "But there are only two copies that I know of."

"Let me guess," said Artie, "one of them is in the stolen book."

"Worse. The true direction spells are in both stolen

books. One copy is in the book that is with Stous. The other is in a book that was stolen recently from the ancient library. This sort of thing is why I posted more guards around my library."

Artie punched his fist in his open hand. "Drat! And I suppose no one knows who's stolen the second book?"

Liam smiled. "I have a guess. An educated guess, at least. I heard Lord Mason say that one of the minions has made it through to the children's realm."

"That's right," Artie said. "Well, he would have needed magic to do that. Since Stous doesn't share, I'm certain he didn't get the spell from the first book." Artie jumped to his feet and grinned, "Liam, you're a genius!"

The elf turned to Dragonfly who was busying herself looking over Lord Mason's battle maps.

"You said you can travel to the children's realm, right?" Artie said.

Dragonfly nodded both heads and Artie set about explaining Liam's theory about the second book stolen from the Ancient Library. She agreed to travel there and search for Rhinosorous.

Dragonfly grinned. "I have tracked him before. I doubt he can lose me in their realm any more easily," "I will go, and I will find that book."

Dragonfly wrapped her wings and began her spinning trick. A few swift turns, and she was gone.

Chapter 11

-Children's Realm-

Dragonfly arrived silently in Christopher's room. Shadows of swiveling heads were cast onto the wall in the yellowish light as she took in the strange look of this realm. It was beautiful in its own way, with everything made from hard surfaces and straight lines so unusual in Cloud Kingdom. On one wall were several pictures of the child called Christopher. On the floor lay several round orbs with laces that reminded Dragonfly of the balls used to play cloud games. There was even a box that showed moving, talking pictures as if it were a stage for tiny people.

Satisfied that Rhinosorous wasn't in the room, Dragonfly crept quietly to the bedroom door. She had to be careful. This was the weak point where she could get caught by a waiting Rhinosorous or by a human. Neither would be welcome. She peeked into the hallway.

The coast was clear. She went ahead cautiously. Her first step triggered a squeaking floor. Dragonfly froze. Gracie turned to the left as Giuliana turned to the right. Nothing. She quickly scooted into the next room, and from the decorations inside, she decided it must be Leah's room.

Dragonfly scanned the room and spotted a closed door, a closet. She drew her sword from her belt and slid the door open. She grinned at what was inside: a sleeping Rhinosorous curled up on the floor. Dragonfly jabbed him in the butt, sending the creature leaping to his feet, his fists swinging wildly through the air. Dragonfly ducked in time to miss his punch, then placed the tip of her sword at his throat. "Calm down, or I'll take off your head before you can say 'Rhinosorous.'"

"What?" he gasped. "Who are you? How do you know who I am?"

"Doesn't matter. The only thing you should be worried about is what happens to you next. Will you be set free, or will I remove that ugly head of yours?"

Rhinosorous heaved a deep breath. "Okay! I'll do whatever you want. I've been trapped here in this realm and I just want out of here. With my head still attached!"

Dragonfly grinned. "You stole something, and I want it back."

"Be more specific; I've stolen a lot of things," the creature whimpered.

"A spell book. I'm sure you used it to get here."

"Yes, fine! I'll hand it over. Just promise not to kill me. Now, get me out of this place!"

"I'll definitely take you back to Cloud Kingdom. And you'll be alive. Otherwise, you wouldn't be able to answer for your crimes before the Council."

Rhinosorous produced the small book of spells and held it firmly in both hands. "It's right here. However, before you take me to stand trial, I have some information that you might want. I'll tell you everything if you don't turn me in."

"You'll tell me everything, regardless," said Dragonfly, pricking his skin with her sword. "I don't feel like being here any more than you do and I'm leaning in the direction of just taking your head back. I'm running out of patience."

"Okay, okay! Back that thing off me before you do

take my head off. When I was using the spell to get to this realm, I saw a few other realms on the way. One of them was Pridosorous, the one with the mazes. When I was there, I saw Egosorous, alive and well."

Dragonfly grunted dismissively and snatched the book from Rhinosorous's hands. It wasn't the book she'd been hunting for hundreds of years, but it brought her one step closer.

"Come on," said Rhinosorous. "That information has to buy me something."

Dragonfly smiled. "It did. It just paid for your trip to the Council."

Chapter 12

- Plans in Action -

Stous stomped back and forth across his war room, shaking the glowing ball in his claw so violently that he nearly tossed it through the cloud opening. He had just watched firsthand everything going on in the children's realm—the continuing treachery of Rhinosorous and the loss of another spell book that should have been his.

One useful bit of information had come from Dragonfly's capture of Stous's minion. Stous could use Egosorous to get to the Council. Without delay, he commanded his minions to seek out his general in the realm of Mirrored Clouds.

"Bring Prous back to me at once. We have much to discuss."

Dragonfly retrieved Rhinosorous and escorted him into the council chamber at sword point. The defeated creature looked almost happy to be back among the clouds despite his circumstances. At the roundtable, Queen Ciella, Lord Mason, Artie, Leah, and Christopher awaited their arrival.

"I've recovered the spell book, as well as the minion," Dragonfly announced, "although I doubt he'll be cooperative."

Artie grinned and cracked his knuckles, "Oh, that won't be a problem. Liam has taught me an interesting new spell while you were gone." Artie floated over to Rhinosorous and reached out a glowing hand. He touched it to the creature's chest directly over his heart and repeated the words he'd learned. "There," said Artie, "now he'll cooperate. He should be incredibly open to the idea of helping us now."

Rhinosorous looked around the room blankly for a moment and then smiled.

Stous watched this through the eyes of Giuliana using his magic orb, his rage over the minion's capture gone.

Rhinosorous wasn't of much use anyway, and he would be even less useful to the cloud people.

He had already set his own plan in motion by planting the false map in Dragonfly's mind—one of them, at least—and now he'd devised another cunning use for her. He opened his connection to her thoughts and compelled Giuliana to seek out Egosorous.

"There's something else," he watched her say to the Council. "This one mentioned something about Egosorous, another minion, hiding out in Pridosorous. He could be useful to us and a danger if we plan to confront Stous in that realm."

"Hmm, good point," Queen Ciella replied. "Can you retrieve him without raising too much suspicion?"

Stous turned to his general, recently summoned from Pridosorous. "Prous," he growled. "You showed Egosorous the territories of Pridosorous. Now you can tell me precisely where to find him."

"I can, and I will," he said bowing to Stous.

Prous quickly gave directions and landmarks to his

master, and Stous relayed them through the magic orb.

Within the glowing ball, Dragonfly spoke to the queen. "I'm not sure why, but I have a feeling I know exactly where to find Egosorous."

"Then capture him," the queen commanded, "and bring him here quickly. We must finish preparing for the ultimate battle."

Stous was impressed with his own cunning, so much so that he laughed openly. His roaring was so wild that even Prous took a step back from the jagged teeth and foul breath.

"Go, quickly!" Stous commanded. "Get back to Egosorous and wait. The Dragonfly will be upon him in minutes!"

As Prous flew from the door to follow his commands, Stous grinned in satisfaction. Now, he couldn't lose. Prous would have his chance to destroy the Dragonfly; if he failed, she would live on to be his messenger to Egosorous. Either way, he would have one more ally or one less enemy.

Dragonfly appeared deep within the maze of Pridosorous, in a corridor that seemed all too much like a piece of Stratocloudous. It was no wonder that Stous's minion would choose such a place to hide out.

"Hello, Dragonfly," a strange voice came from behind her.

Dragonfly twirled to respond. She was too slow. Before she could dodge out of the way, Prous leaped onto her with giant, netlike arms. Like beautiful spider webs, the nets entwined her from head to toe, making it impossible for her to move.

"Let me go!"

Prous ignored her pleas and leaned in close. Sweeping his tongue across his bared teeth, he whispered into Giuliana's ear, "You've served Stous well, but now you're mine!" Prous laughed, tightening his nets around his prey. "Whether you know it or not, you've served. Stous placed a spell on you, making you Stous's spy. He sees what you see, hears what you hear."

Giuliana gasped, realizing what had happened during their battle in the Valley of Distrust. Knowing the amount of damage she could have done by serving as Stous's eyes and ears, filled Giuliana with rage. With a burst of renewed power, Dragonfly spread her wings, breaking Prous's hold enough for Gracie to unsheathe her sword. The blade sliced through the net as soon as it left its scabbard, and freed Dragonfly from the bonds.

Prous grunted and reared back as his nets fell free. He retreated quickly.

Gracie returned the sword to her belt. "What came over you? I've never seen you so angry. And what was he mumbling about Stous seeing what you see?"

"I…I was just angry. I don't like being trapped in nets," Giuliana said.

Gracie nodded, still confused but resolute.

"We've come this far. Let's find Egosorous and get out of here," Gracie replied.

Giuliana nodded but suddenly felt a tingling in her head. Thoughts came to her slowly, as if from another world. They were difficult to understand fully, but she could swear it sounded like, "Give this message to Egosorous."

Chapter 13

-Message to Egosorous-

Dragonfly navigated the maze quickly and quietly so as not to draw attention to herself, although there was hardly a soul to be found in Pridosorous. The way was more confusing than they'd hoped, although Giuliana still seemed to know where to find Egosorous.

"We should be close. At least, I think we should," Giuliana said, looking up at the reflected version of the realm above. "Wait!" she whispered suddenly. "Up there!" said Giuliana.

By sheer luck, she'd spotted Egosorous's reflection overhead. Dragonfly moved quickly, sword drawn, to catch him.

"This is where this realm gets tricky," said Gracie, looking skyward.

They would have to jump to the reflection to close distance. Dragonfly leaped upwards, flipped like a mirror image, misjudged, and collided with a solid stretch of cloud wall. Tumbling and falling to the sound of Egosorous's cackling, Dragonfly landed flat on her back right where she'd started.

"Gracie," Giuliana said, looking to her left. "Gracie!"

Gracie was completely unconscious. Giuliana reached over and touched Gracie's cheek, but her head did not move.

"Just leave her," Egosorous said, looming over them. "I'll take care of her as soon as I'm finished with you."

"Wait!" Giuliana shouted. "I have a message from Stous! He says that he knows Rhinosorous is the traitor and that he was wrong to banish you." Again, her head tingled, and the words flowed out of her from some unknown source.

"What do you know of Stous?" Egosorous growled.

"I'm his eyes and ears. He's watching you right now through a spell. I'm sure you wouldn't want to harm a messenger from Stous. Not after he's invited you back to stand by his side."

These words were entirely Giuliana's, spoken only to persuade the foul minion to allow her and Gracie to live.

Egosorous stared down at Dragonfly for a long minute, weighing the joy of ending her life against the risk of once again angering Stous. "Bah!" he said. "Leave me. Be gone."

Dragonfly rose unsteadily to her feet, making shaky preparations to go.

"Wait," Egosorous stepped up and looked Giuliana square in the eyes. "If Stous is truly in there, then let him know that I live to serve him. I will stand by his side."

Giuliana's head lowered, partly in shame, partly in defeat, as she used every remaining bit of her power to wrap her wings, spin, and disappear.

"Send word I would like to see Egosorous," Stous bellowed.

Egosorous stood before Stous's throne.

"I shouldn't have judged you so quickly," Stous said.

"Why did you then?"

Stous snorted and dismissed the question. "Now, we must agree to put that behind us for the ultimate battle that is coming."

"What makes you think I would put this behind me?"

"Come, make yourself comfortable in my war room," said Stous, gesturing to a place at his side.

"I want to serve," said Egosorous, fighting to keep his voice firm, "but to serve you, I must trust you."

Stous sneered. "You will see that I am a master that can be trusted."

"When the time comes, you will see."

Chapter 14

-*Reports to Council*-

Several days passed and the realms fell deeper into turmoil. With the Dinosorous Games behind them, the cloud folk lost much of their cheer. More cloud folk were being moved from their homes, and more of Stous's minions were taking up residence in their homes.

Knowing that their time was running short, the Council met for what they knew might be the last time. Within Cloud Castle, the members of the Council took seats at the roundtable. This included Queen Ciella, Lord Mason, Liam, the Librarian, Artie, the Elf, Dragonfly, no longer stumbling from her run-in with Prous, Captain Christopher, and Commander Leah. Turning, Artie called for two more chairs to be added to the roundtable. Bowing with respect, Artie welcomed Oda and Paola.

"Attention," the queen called. "Let us hear the final reports. The time for action has never been nearer."

Dragonfly stood first, hand on the hilt of her sword, and spoke. "As you know, we've captured Rhinosorous and retrieved the second stolen book. I've created the map of Pridosorous, as Artie asked. Egosorous remains at large, and we assume has reunited with his master." Dragonfly returned to her seat.

"How are your wounds, Dragonfly?" asked Lord Mason.

"They've healed well enough. I stand ready for the battle to come."

Lord Mason nodded.

Artie stood. "Our scouting party found an ideal battleground for facing Stous. Pridosorous. Even though it's dangerous, we've prepared well for the task." Artie grinned. "Now, before I explain…" With a flourish, the elf clapped his hands together, creating a massive shower of sparks. The sparks whirled and spun around the room, growing, and took on the form of a comet. Without warning, the comet broke off from its rotation and hit Giuliana right in the forehead, causing her head to fall limp.

"What have you done?" screamed Gracie, drawing

her sword. "I should take your head for that!"

The rest of the Council sat silently in disbelief, only stirring to action when Artie waved his arm and put Dragonfly back into her chair with the force of magic.

"That's quite enough, Artie!" scowled Queen Ciella. "I don't know what you presume—"

"If you'll forgive me, your majesty," Artie cut in, "but that needed to be done." He looked over to Dragonfly, squirming violently in her chair. "I'm sorry, Gracie. But Giuliana was under a spell. Stous has been using her as his eyes and ears, spying on our every move."

Gracie's eyes widened and she stopped struggling with the magical force.

"When I whispered into your ear, it was a test," said Artie. "After you were ambushed by Prous and Egosorous, I was nearly certain. They knew exactly where you would be, and only because Stous saw everything firsthand. Then I received a secret message that confirmed my suspicions. What was most curious is that I believe the news came from Egosorous."

All heads turned to Artie.

"Why would he do that?" Liam asked.

"I believe Egosorous is planning his own takeover and he'll use anyone to help himself." Artie released the bond and Dragonfly fell limp into her chair.

"It makes sense now," Gracie said. "When we were battling Prous, Giuliana said, 'He sees what I see and hears what I hear.'"

"Then you understand," Artie said solemnly. "But now we can be free of his spying. She'll be okay in a few hours, and when she comes to, she will no longer be under Stous's control."

Gracie thought for a moment, then spoke. "The maps. The maps we drew of Pridosorous. Giuliana kept telling me to change things, accusing me of remembering wrong.

"That was Stous, trying to set traps for us by tampering with the map. We won't be using them."

"Then how will we ever find our way into that place?" asked Leah.

"Liam has found the spells needed to navigate the maze within the book that Dragonfly recovered."

Christopher raised his hand, chiming in. "Artie, I'm

still a bit confused about that realm. It still doesn't seem like a safe place to face Stous."

"Christopher, we have the true direction spell from the second book thanks to Dragonfly. And if Gracie would be so kind, she can draw us a new map without Stous's influence to sabotage it."

Christopher nodded.

"Of course, I will. It won't take long this time," said Gracie. "I'm sorry, I should have known."

"You couldn't have known," said Queen Ciella.

"Stous is a dark and manipulative fiend," Lord Mason said. "Is it safe to speak of the battle plan?"

"It is," Artie replied.

Lord Mason stood. "I have studied the false map well enough to understand that Stous was setting his minions at various points to ambush us. As soon as Gracie draws the accurate map, I will know exactly where his minions are positioned. My warriors will root them out at once before the main attack."

"Excellent," said Queen Ciella. "Then as soon as the map is drawn, Lord Mason and I will summon our armies. Then, we move."

Leah jumped to her feet and cheered, "It's time to finish this!"

Chapter 15

Battle Cry

The call to arms began as a whisper from Queen Ciella. The time had come. One by one, they filed out to the top of the tallest parapet tower in Cloud Castle. Once again, the companions known as the Council peered out over the vast expanse of the kingdoms. The stars created pinholes in the curtain of dark sky that lit the black night.

"Today we fight for freedom." said Lord Mason.

Artie turned from the glorious view and placed his hand in front of him. Each council member followed in turn, one hand on top of the other. Queen Ciella first, then Lord Mason, Dragonfly, Liam, Christopher, Leah, Oda, and Paola. From the parapets, Elephantous and Aero kept guard.

"We do this because duty calls," said Artie, "and we are doers!"

Raising their hands above their heads, everyone

shouted in unison, "Until the end!"

Trumpeting, Elephantous followed Aero as they flew a circle around the Council. A moment later, when the cheers calmed down, the weight of the situation returned.

Queen Ciella began the marching orders. "We must begin. Liam, Lord Mason, Oda, and Paola will travel with me on the Rainbow Causeway. Dragonfly, you have your way of getting through to these realms so we will meet you there. Artie, the captain, and the commander will travel with Aero and Elephantous. Liam, you will need to set us up and synchronize us."

"Prepare!" shouted Liam, once again positioning each of the council members to synchronize their sense of time. "Now!" he shouted.

And they were gone.

Christopher held himself firmly against the harsh winds that had blown into the realm. He and the others had been in Pridosorous only days ago, but it had not been this unwelcoming. Now, the sky was dark purple, and branches of lightning broke overhead continually.

"This place seems wrong," said Leah with a shiver.

"It always seemed wrong," Christopher said in a wry tone.

"You know what I mean."

Beside them on Aero, Artie stared ahead in silence. Christopher assumed he was worried about the others. They were the first, and so far, the only members of the Council to arrive in Pridosorous.

Just as Christopher was about to share his concerns that something terrible had happened to the rest of their friends, Dragonfly appeared before them with a flourish. She was dressed head to toe in full battle regalia and heavily armored, sword in hand. Adorned like the princess she was, the others looked on in awe. She peered toward the three companions aboard the floating magic carpet and bowed, moving into battle formation.

Artie smiled. "Ah, now that you're here, I can invite your friend."

The elf clapped, and with a flash of light, Rhinosorous appeared before them looking mildly confused.

"What's he doing here?" asked Christopher.

Artie grinned. "It never hurts to have a decoy."

The rest of the landing party descended and took up their positions.

Chapter 16

-First and Last Trip-

Stous was fed up with the glowing ball in his claw that no longer fed him the sights and sounds of Dragonfly's mind. "Worthless!" he growled, crushing the orb into magic dust.

Egosorous stepped into the chamber, taking note of the destroyed orb as the shards drifted to the floor. "Good news," he said with a bow. "Your magic ball may not be of much use now, but what it has already told you has proven valuable. The fools have arrived in Pridosorous, just as they discussed."

"Then they will fall into my traps after all: the false maps, the waiting minions. They will either be slain or lost in that maze for eternity." Stous snickered, his nostrils widening. Puffs of putrid vapor rose from them.

"And what about the child creatures?" asked Egosorous.

Stous grinned and held out his claw. Wrapped around it was a golden chain, and from that chain dangled half an amulet. "I believe that this will lead me right to them. The battle is about to begin. Go, fetch my spell book."

Egosorous rushed from the chamber and returned cradling the precious book of incantations.

"I must only read from these spells," said Stous, opening the book to a well-worn page, "and it will open a portal to the children. It should be much easier to travel to Pridosorous than when I tried to reach them in their own realm."

Egosorous said nothing. He looked on as Stous began to recite the incantation from the page. He didn't understand the words, but he could tell that the same lines were repeated over and over as Stous chanted them louder and louder. As he did so, a portal began to shimmer and split in the air in front of Stous. The words continued, echoing off into the distance, and the gateway grew broader and brighter. Suddenly, the heavens echoed with a thunderous sound of the magic bracelet that tethered Stous snapping. Stous's escape was complete. When the entrance became large enough, Stous dropped the book and leaped through without a word. An instant later, Stous appeared on the other side of the portal. Looking around, he saw the tall cloud walls of the maze. Dark clouds thundered all around but he knew he was no longer in Stratocloudous.

"Ah ha!" Stous laughed, holding the amulet high in the air. "At last! I'm free, and this realm will be the perfect place to launch my conquest of all the realms and beyond!"

Chapter 17

- The Battle Begins -

Artie suddenly appeared atop Aero, causing Leah and Christopher to cease staring at the endless stretch of the maze around them. Queen Ciella and Lord Mason and the rest of the Council had since joined them, floating at their side. Then they all seemed to shudder.

"He's here," Artie said, glaring into the distance.

"I felt him too," said Dragonfly. "It's like the air just got colder. Much colder."

"Stous is free of Stratocloudous," whispered Queen Ciella.

Leah wanted to gasp, but she stilled herself. This was all part of their plan.

"As soon as we see Stous," Artie told Dragonfly, "you must travel to Stratocloudous and steal back the book…

that is, if we don't see it in his hands."

"I stand ready," said Dragonfly.

Artie grinned. "While you're there, can you just lay waste to that godforsaken place?"

Dragonfly grinned back. "I will do my best to leave it in ruins."

"Queen Ciella, when you and Lord Mason take your positions in the maze, bring Rhinosorous with you," said Artie.

"That seems foolhardy," said Lord Mason.

"Not at all," Artie said, pointing to the battle map. "Take him to this turn and release him. This is where Egosorous will be positioned."

Lord Mason smiled. "Ah, they will not be happy to see each other."

"That's right. Let Egosorous and Rhinosorous fight it out. It will be to the death, most likely. You will only need to finish the one left standing. Now, go. We will set a trap for Stous."

Artie watched as the Council led Rhinosorous into

the turns of the maze.

Lord Mason peered around the corner and quickly drew back his head. Turning to Queen Ciella, he nodded. "Egosorous is near."

"This is where your fate has brought you," Queen Ciella said to Rhinosorous. "Now, go!"

Rhinosorous rounded the corner, at once spotting Egosorous. Without hesitation, he charged. Egosorous turned at the sound of thundering feet but was too late. The stunning blow sent him flying to the ground.

With a scream of pain, Egosorous fought to stand up, cursing the treacherous Rhinosorous. Again, with another spine-crunching blow, Egosorous was knocked aside. He barely kept his ground. Rhinosorous rose to his hind legs, ready to drop the fatal blow, but Egosorous rolled deftly out of the way. With a mighty leap, he was back on his feet with sword in hand, and Rhinosorous's eyes widened with surprise.

"Ha! You have not learned to think more than one move ahead," shouted Egosorous. "It will be your downfall."

The two clashed as if dancing with Egosorous,

swinging, and slashing his sword. Rhinosorous managed to dodge each time. Finally, Egosorous charged in with a brutal thrust, the blade of his sword driving deep into his opponent. Rhinosorous's blood spray-painted the clouds behind him.

"Why are you grinning, you fool?" Egosorous growled.

"This time," choked Rhinosorous, "I did think ahead."

Looking down, Egosorous saw that his opponent had drawn a dagger and that Rhinosorous had buried it deep into his side.

As the pain rushed in and the smell of blood rose, Egosorous screeched and rocketed skyward, disappearing into the reflected clouds as lightning flashed overhead.

Below, Rhinosorous collapsed to the ground and took his last breath, while Lord Mason and Queen Ciella cursed at missing their chance to rid the realms of Egosorous.

Attuned to the battle, Artie was now ready. He reached out to Leah. "May I have your half of the amulet please?"

She placed it in his hand.

"Thank you." He stepped back and held the amulet in front of him.

Christopher and Leah watched as the elf whispered into the amulet, his words causing it to glow with magical power and bob in the air above his hands. Seconds later, a cloud of dust rolled toward them at breakneck speed, coming to a stop directly in front of Artie. When the dust settled they saw Stous, battered and bruised, with the other half of the amulet wrapped around his claw. The wicked creature stood up without wasting a second and stared defiantly at each of them in turn.

"Well, well. It seems the amulet did bring me to you: the two child creatures and their little protector."

Leah clenched her fists and shouted, "We don't need a protector from the likes of you!"

Christopher reached out and placed his arm on his sister's shoulder to hold her back. "Just wait. I want to see Artie bait Stous."

Artie never took his eyes off Stous. With a sly grin, he nodded towards the creature's deformed claw. "I see you never recovered from that little wound I gave you," Artie said.

Stous growled and charged wildly at Artie. The elf sidestepped the attack, and Stous slid to a teetering halt behind him.

"You're going to have a tough time hitting me with just one eye. Didn't you lose that eye to one of the cloud people?" Artie chuckled. "If I remember, he wasn't even a warrior, just a kid who wandered away from the playground. That must be embarrassing."

Captain Christopher and Commander Leah watched on in amusement.

Fired up with fierce rage, Stous lost any composure that remained and charged once more with a furious roar. This time, Artie struck him in the side as he passed, knocking the wind out of him. Stous stumbled to his feet. His eye caught something behind the elf and he roared with laughter showing off rows of jagged teeth.

"You have a strange sense of humor," quipped Artie, "or do you always laugh when you know you've been defeated?"

"Not quite, elf," smiled Stous. "Look behind you."

"Not on your life."

Stous replaced his sword in his sheath, raised his hands, and repeated, "Look behind."

"Why should I believe you?"

"Look, I have put up my sword." Once again, he stretched out his hands. "I will honor you with no attack."

Chapter 18

The Battle Takes a Wrong Turn –

Artie looked over his shoulder, and his heart sank. Behind him, Leah and Christopher were trapped inside the netlike arms of one of Stous's minions, Prous. Both struggled against their captor but were helpless.

"Before you try anything," Stous continued, "know that if you make a move, the children will be done for. Prous has them locked up tight, but he can squeeze them much, much harder."

Artie glared back at Stous and then returned his gaze to Prous and his net. "Do what you want with me," he said, "but let them go. Let them go back to their own realm in peace."

Stous ignored the elf and walked toward him. With one swipe of his claw, he knocked Artie to the ground, sending the other half of the amulet flying from his pocket. Stous caught it with his free hand.

"Christopher!" shouted Leah. "The amulet!"

Christopher understood. He reached out his hand, and shouted, "Amulet! Assemble and return to your rightful owner!"

With those words, both halves of the amulet began to shake and spin through the air. They moved with such speed that the chains broke each of Stous's claws, shredding them to pieces as both halves flew together to reunite in Christopher's hand. Stous himself fell to the ground in pain as Prous watched on in horror. Artie saw his chance, rose to his knees, and clapped his hands together. A thunderous blast and flash of lightning tore through Prous's net, setting the adventurers free. Their freedom wasn't yet secured, as Egosorous dropped from the sky as suddenly as they had been released. With one swift motion, Egosorous winked at Artie then blasted him with a cloud ball that sent the elf flying halfway across the realm.

"Excellent work, Egosorous," said Stous, choking through the pain of his destroyed claws. "When this is over, you will help me rule over all the realms."

Egosorous beamed a crooked smile, but Prous looked furious.

"What about me?" he yelled. "I saved you first!"

Stous grinned at Prous. "Well, of course, you'll rule beside me."

Stous swaggered over to the child creatures. Tilting his good phosphorescent eye, he tortured them slowly with his stare. With a mangled claw, he reached up and swiped the amulet from Christopher's hand. Drops of blood and foul stains streaked Christopher's clothing as the claw withdrew.

When Lord Mason and Queen Ciella appeared from the maze, they were stunned to see Artie lying bruised on the ground.

"Artie!" Queen Ciella gasped. "Are you all right?"

The elf slowly stood, his hands on his head and his knees shaking. "I'll be okay, just a little ego bruising, but Stous has the kids. Something hit me with such force it blasted me halfway across the realm."

"The battle inside the maze is won," said Lord Mason,

"and Stous's minions are on the run. But he won't rest until we're all gone, and he knows that the Council still stands."

"That's right," Queen Ciella agreed. "I'm sure he will use the children to bait us. We must simply wait for him to set a trap and then turn the tide against him."

Artie sighed, disappointed in the last-minute failure of a well-laid plan. "What about Dragonfly?" he asked. "Please tell me that she at least got the book."

Queen Ciella shook her head. "We don't know. Dragonfly has not yet returned."

"Well, let's hope she's having better luck than I am."

After leading his minions and his captives back to his new war room on Pridosorous, Stous wondered how best to use them to his advantage.

"We can send a message with our demands," suggested Prous.

"Yes," Stous nodded. "I'll tell them that I'll trade the children's lives for the lives of the rest of their Council. Prous, do you have any more of your nets to capture them?"

"No, but it won't take me long to spin some more."

"Do it," Stous ordered. "And Egosorous, you will stand ready on the front lines with your cloud weapons. Be prepared."

Both minions bowed and set about their tasks.

It did not take long for Stous's messenger to deliver his master's demands. Lord Mason received the note at the gates of Cloud Kingdom and hurried it to the council chamber.

"It's as we expected. Stous wants us in exchange for the children."

"And he most certainly won't let any of us live one way or another," said Artie.

Chapter 19

The Tables Turn

"We must spring Stous's trap and hope that we can turn it against him," said Queen Ciella.

"He still has the amulets," said Artie, "which is in our favor. I can call upon the magic in the amulet to create a protective field around Leah and Christopher, the true bearers of the amulet's power."

"Good," Lord Mason cut in, "and once they're safe, we can attack."

"I will strike Stous," said Artie. "Queen Ciella, you can finish Egosorous. That leaves Prous for you, Lord Mason."

All nodded and just as they set off toward the gates, another of Stous's messengers floated down from above. In its hands, it looked to be holding three of Prous's nets.

"Tell your master that we're making the trade," roared Lord Mason, pointing toward the gate. "We were just leaving."

The messenger cackled, "Not that way, I'm afraid. Stous insists that you slip into these. He doesn't quite trust you to stick to the deal."

Leaning in to whisper in Queen Ciella's ear, Artie said, "If we confront Stous wrapped up in nets, all hope is lost."

"We have no choice," Queen Ciella said back. "We must do as he says or the children stand no chance."

One by one, the three slipped into the nets. Once tied tightly, the messenger floated them back to the main chamber. The cave entrance seemed to swallow up all sunlight. The dankness of the cave covered their skin like hundreds of bugs crawling over them.

The messenger was not gentle in his treatment of the three, dropping them on the hard, cold, wet chamber floor right at the feet of Egosorous.

As Artie landed, he whispered to Queen Ciella, "When the time is right, can you use your talons to cut these nets."

"No, I'm in no position to reach them."

"Quiet!" Egosorous bellowed.

Artie, Lord Mason, and Queen Ciella struggled within the nets, but only made it worse. They could not escape. The nets just grew tighter as they wiggled and fought against them. Egosorous laughed heartily at the captive Council members helpless before him.

"I wouldn't laugh just yet," grunted Lord Mason. "Stous trusts no one and shares nothing. Whatever he promised you, you'll never see it."

Egosorous roared and kicked Lord Mason. then grabbed Artie and pulled him up off the ground. He looked straight into Artie's eyes and secretly poked him in the side with his dagger. Egosorous laughed in Artie's face, dropped the blade into his pocket, and threw the elf to the ground.

They looked about the chamber. Chains hung from the walls with blood still dripping from the torture devices. They heard rumblings and cackling in the next room over.

"Prous, you keep these three here," Egosorous ordered.

Stous marched into his war room where he had the child creatures bound and ready for execution. Stous himself was holding a sword in one mangled claw, the point leveled squarely at the two children beside him. With the lust of death in his eyes, Stous grinned. He was nearly shaking with excitement at his victory. "Egosorous, what took you so long? I've been waiting for those miserable Council members," Stous bellowed.

Egosorous sauntered over to the minion standing next to Stous and commanded, "Move over. I stand next to Stous and you stand next to me."

Grumbling and glaring, the minion moved. Egosorous moved closer to Stous. He steadied himself to plunge his dagger into Stous at the right moment.

Prous wrenched the nets and dropped all three Council members to the floor. As they hit the floor, they heard the swoop and slash of the sword and the inevitable thud of heads hitting the ground.

Queen Ciella, horrified by the vision of the heads of those two beautiful children being severed from their bodies, shook with rage. Raising her fist in the air, she cried, "Stous, you shall pay for this with your life."

Lord Mason let out a loud moan and growl that shook

the cave walls.

Artie grabbed his chest, fell to one knee, and screamed, "CURSE YOU, Stous."

Prous laughed with delight, "Get up, you're next. Stous is waiting in his war room. Get moving."

As Artie struggled to get up, he tried to trip Prous but to no avail. The cavern door creaked open as the rodents scurried out of the way. Stous's ominous shadow brought the scent of blood into the room.

Prous bowed. "Oh master, I was just bringing them to you."

When Artie saw Stous, he charged forward tripping on his net only to fall flat on his face. Lord Mason roared at the sight of Stous. Queen Ciella tried a magic spell that did not work.

"No need to." Stous gleefully walked around the Council. "It's so good to see all of you again," Stous mocked.

The Council lowered their heads from the foul odor emanating from Stous.

The drool slithered down his teeth as his tongue tried

to slurp it back up. With a voice as cold and sharp as a double-edged sword, Stous said quivering, "Oh, how I have waited to see you on your knees before me. Stous stepped forward and planted his massive leg for the killing stroke. With his sword in both hands, he swung down toward the Council with all his force.

With a loud clash of metal, the sword stopped mid-strike. The power caused the sword to crash to the ground as it was wrenched from Stous's mangled claws. As quick as a clap of thunder, Dragonfly swooped down in front of Stous, sword in hand. She knocked the Council members clear into the war chamber.

Stous reached for his sword and said angrily, "I'll have your head for that."

"Not so fast," a sing-song voice said. "I still owe you something!"

Stous backed up and charged forward in a rage. He approached Gracie's blindside and delivered a smashing blow. Dragonfly's sword missed her mark as her knees buckled. Artie took the dagger that Egosorous gave him, and with a few quick flicks of the knife, cut the nets that held his friends. Queen Ciella pounced on Stous, dragging her claws down his massive torso. Stous curled one wing inward to cover the gigantic holes in his chest.

"Come here, you little jackal," Stous said, giving chase to Queen Ciella.

"Great timing, Dragonfly." Artie grabbed her and settled her down. "I'll take it from here."

Dragonfly handed Artie the sword and his magical chest. He looked up with a smile of thanks.

Stous clamped a hand around Queen Ciella. Lord Mason pounced on Stous with a ferocious bite to his neck. He let go of Queen Ciella, reached back, ripped Lord Mason off his back, and threw him. Stous retreated and started reciting an incantation. Dragonfly stepped aside as Artie grew to accommodate Stous's large sword.

Artie picked up the massive sword and charged forward only to do a double take. His heart soared as he yelled, "Christopher, Leah, you're alive. Lord Mason, Queen Ciella, they're alive."

Stous finished his incantation. "Now, come to me, my minions."

Prous dove into the chamber at his master's call, but

Lord Mason stood between them. Lord Mason drew his sword and with a single stroke, removed the creature's head. Without so much as a gasp, a headless Prous fell limp on top of Egosorous and his minion.

The space below swirled into a funnel that opened into a portal with Christopher, Leah, Artie, and Stous tumbling through, arms and feet scrambling for a foothold that would not come. Their weapons fell from their hands as they tried to stop themselves from falling.

Leah thought she recognized the screaming voices of her mother and father as she and Christopher, dressed in pirate garb, crashed through the ceiling of their home onto the living room floor.

"What is that?" Leah heard her mom say in complete disbelief as an elven creature dressed in battle armor crashed to the floor beside her daughter. Other strange and colorful things fell out of nowhere also.

Stunned and frightened by the ungodly sound wrenching through their ceiling, her dad and mom had jumped out of their seats. "Christopher! Leah! What... how...?" her parents stuttered. Leah cringed as Stous plummeted into the room before any of them could begin to make sense of what was going on.

"Mom! Dad!" Leah cried protectively, but she could see her dad's military training kick in, and, without a moment's hesitation, he jumped onto Stous's back. Stous bellowed so loud the walls shook, pictures fell, and the curtains danced on his hot putrid breath. A creature of immense strength, Stous flipped her dad over his head and onto the floor, raising one of his massive legs to drive it down on her father.

"No," screamed Leah's mom.

Christopher rushed to rescue his father, knocking him out of the way just as Stous's foot came down. Enraged by the boy's interference, Stous grew to his full height. He took his enormous mangled claw and backhanded Christopher across the room. Christopher seemed to bend in half as the blow pounded him into the far wall. He fell lifeless to the floor. A sudden collective gasp filled the room; then it went silent.

The house rumbled as Stous stomped his way toward Christopher, removing his sword for the final blow. The shaft of an arrow glimmered in the sunlight as it flew across the room and hit its mark. Stous screeched as the arrow took out his seeing eye. The next arrow pierced his chest, exposing Stous's blackened heart, as a red fire consumed him from the inside out before his body even hit the floor. The amulet lay in a pile of ashes on the floor.

A shocked Leah watched as her dad picked up her brother and cradled him in his arms, rocking him, as her mom hovered over them, both crying wretchedly. Leah ran to Christopher's side screaming, "Christopher, hold on please, please," as hot tears streamed down her cheeks too.

It hurt Artie's heart to hear them. He grabbed the amulets and disappeared.

Christopher's dad checked Christopher's pulse. "Call 911," he said quietly to his wife.

With a flash of stardust, Artie appeared at their side. He reached into his cloak as he looked into Leah's eyes. "I don't know if this elixir will work in your realm."

Mom, Dad, and Leah gathered around Artie and Christopher as Artie anointed Christopher's body. A bright orange aura appeared.

"Look, it's working," Leah said.

The orange aura sizzled and phased in and out. Leah grabbed Artie with all her might and shook him. "What's happening?" she screamed.

Artie peered into the slits of Christopher's eyes, as they fluttered for what looked like the last time. "You can't leave us now. You can do this. Come back!" Christopher's young body thrashed about.

"Christopher, wake up. Please!" his mother wailed in desperation, while his dad sobbed over and over, "Son, you saved my life. You saved my life."

Leah threw her arms around him. "Christopher, I believe in you! You must come back. BROTHER!"

A portal ripped open above them and the kids' parents raised their eyes to the ceiling, aghast at what they saw. The Council was descending. Artie looked up to see Queen Ciella, Lord Mason, Prince Nolan, Liam the Librarian, and Dragonfly. They extended their hands out as they called out to Christopher. Ripples in the atmosphere carried an unnatural light toward the boy from which echoed an incantation. "We infuse you with the combined strength of the Council. Awaken!"

Also, a barely perceptible phosphorescent light that shown from behind the members mingled with their incantation as it struck Christopher and his eyes fluttered open. Christopher sat up. "What's going on?" he asked groggily.

He could hear the fading laughter of the council members as they disappeared through the closing portal.

Christopher's Mom looked at Artie. "Who and what are you?" She grabbed her son and clenched him tight. "What are you doing with my children?"

"All questions will be answered in time. Please, I will need Captain Christopher and Commander Leah for one moment," Artie said

"Oh no, you don't. You'll answer my question first. Who and what are Captain Christopher and Commander Leah?"

"Sorry, but I don't belong to this realm, and thus am not accountable to you. I promise your children are all right and will be back in the blink of an eye. They will then answer all your questions. Christopher and Leah, this will only take a minute."

They nodded their assent and with a flash, the kids were gone. The parents looked at one another wondering what they had just agreed to.

Artie escorted the kids into the castle in Cloud Kingdom. They arrived to loud cheers and jubilation. In the Council chambers, the bruised but victorious members sat at the roundtable. Flowers of every color decorated the chamber and piles of delicious food and drink filled the space that was once home to battle maps.

"I was terrified when I heard that sword come down. I thought you two were goners," Queen Ciella said.

"I as well," said Lord Mason, raising his golden cup. "My heart broke and I lost nearly half of my life essence when I heard that sword come around."

"So what you heard was Stous taking Egosorous's head?" asked Leah.

"Yes, and that of one of his minions.

"Why would he kill Egosorous? I thought he was one of Stous's most valuable minions," said Christopher.

"Egosorous was getting stronger," Artie said. "His powers were a threat to Stous. Lust for power allows for no sharing. There could only be one ruler in Stous's world. He didn't want any competition. Also, Stous might have found out that he was secretly planning to overthrow him, using me for help." Artie reached out and put his hand on Leah's shoulder. "That's why he didn't take your heads off; Stous wanted you and your brother killed in front of us."

"I'm just glad it's all over," said Leah.

"Yes," said Queen Ciella. "Stous is finished and Dragonfly will return both stolen spell books to their rightful kingdoms. Also, all the souls were returned to their rightful bodies, once Stous died."

Oda and Paola raised their cups and cried in unison, "We have heard from the elders who are grateful."

Artie smiled at Dragonfly. "How does it feel to be free of that quest for the first time in centuries?"

"Very good," she replied. "Almost as good as knowing that the evil has been cleansed from the realms."

"Indeed," continued Queen Ciella. "All is right within the realms. We can plan our next meeting to discuss the children's realm. As I recall, Lord Mason has a branch of the Rainbow Causeway that needs to be finished."

Leah and Christopher looked at each other and smiled. With a portal to their world, all sorts of children could come to enjoy the wonders of Cloud Kingdom.

"There will be plenty of questions from your parents when you get back. Would you like me to accompany you?" Artie asked.

"No, we will call you if we need you," Christopher said.

Christopher stretched out his hand and Artie dropped both halves of the amulet into it. Leaning forward, he whispered in Christopher's ear, "I'm proud of you, me boy! You offered up your life to save your father's without hesitation. You have come a long way since our first adventure. I would be proud for you to stand by my side in any battle."

"Thank you," Christopher said. Leah bowed her head as Christopher reached over to place her half of the amulet around her neck.

Turning to Artie, Christopher said, "Thank you for everything, but we really need to return home. Our parents…"

"Yes, yes…" said Artie. "We understand."

Leah smiled and waved. "Good-bye, everyone. We promise to come back soon"

The siblings turned to each other, then grabbed the amulets around their necks, and with a flash disappeared.

Queen Ciella appeared at Artie's side. "When will you tell Christopher that with the healing power bestowed upon him by the Council—the power that saved his life—came the essence of each master, and one day he will be called upon to rule all eight kingdoms?"

Artie smiled and waved as they vanished. Suddenly, he felt a twinge in his body where Stous had wounded him. He paused for a moment and shook his head as a menacing thought went through him. "When the time is right."

Queen Ciella frowned. "Well, don't wait until we're at war again," she said as she sauntered off.

The kids popped into the living room. Surprised, Mom and Dad grabbed their kids, checking for any injuries and then just held them tight.

"Please, please tell me you're both all right," their

Mom cried.

They nodded. "We're fine, Mom," Christopher said.

"Leah?"

"Yes, Mom, I am too. Truly. We're sorry about not telling you about Cloud Kingdom before, but we didn't know how or if you would even believe us."

Sitting on the couch, Christopher and Leah took turns telling their story of Cloud Kingdom and the wondrous realms and characters. After many questions and answers, it was time for bed.

Their parents sent them up to bed and sat quietly together on the sofa for a few minutes. Leah lingered for a moment at the top of the stairs, wondering if her dad and mom had believed any of the stories she and her brother had told them. Then she overheard them talking. "I wouldn't have believed any of it if I hadn't seen it with my own eyes," her dad said.

"Me neither."

"It's late. Let's go to bed."

"Mom, Dad are you coming up to say prayers?" Christopher called down, giving Leah a chance to scramble into her bedroom.

They went first to Leah's room, then quietly closed the door when they were done and finished prayers in Christopher's.

"Stay home tonight! No Cloud Kingdom!" they called to their children as they descended the stairs.

"We need to set up some sort of rules. I need to talk to this Artie fellow," Mom continued.

Christopher laughed. "Yes, Mom, Dad."

"It's not funny, young man. Now, go to sleep."

The morning sun was shining brightly through the kitchen window when Dad walked in the next morning.

"Morning, Christopher. Get dressed. I want to take a walk."

"Okay."

Walking through the woods, his dad asked, "Remember this place?"

"Yes, it's where I lost the new lead pencil you gave me."

"That's right. I want to tell you that I might have jumped to some conclusions about that."

"Yeah?"

"I overreacted."

Christopher offered a slight snicker. "Which part?"

"Well, all of it and I'm sorry about that."

"That's okay, Dad."

"No, it's not. You have changed so much since that bullying incident." Dad grinned. "And you saved my life."

"I learned a lot in Cloud Kingdom. How to handle bullies, teamwork, working with people or creatures that are different from me. You know, Dad, you tried to teach me many of those things, too, but I just wasn't ready to hear them. And for that I am sorry."

Reaching down, Dad rubbed the top of Christopher's head. "I love you, Son. Now there are a few more lessons you'll need to prepare for manhood."

"I'm sure there are, Dad, but not now. Okay?"

"We'll need to discuss this traveling between realms thing."

Christopher laughed. "Yep."

Chapter 20

-*Warasorous*-

Beneath the council chambers in Cloud Kingdom, where the people of the realm were still celebrating, a mass of dark clouds were forming. With all the troubles in the realms, no one had even noticed it. Nor did they see that within the mass of clouds, a new domain was forming. It would be called Warasorous, named for the creature that now stood in the center of the mass— Warous. As his phosphorescent eyes glared at the scene unfolding above, he recited an incantation that his father had taught him before he was lost forever.